RIGHT WITH ME

STACEY LEWIS

LADY BOSS PRESS

KRISTEN PROBY

Right With Me

A With Me In Seattle Universe Novel

By Stacey Lewis

RIGHT WITH ME

A With Me In Seattle Universe Novel

Stacey Lewis

Copyright © 2020 by Stacey Lewis

Cover Design: Kari March

Editing by: AL Edits

Published by Lady Boss Press, Inc.

CHAPTER 1

Mitchell

*A*ll week the shop guys have been talking about the new girl at Patsy's. I'll admit, after hearing how fuckable she is, I'm curious to see how she measures up to their descriptions. That's the only reason I walk over with them. At least, that's what I tell myself.

Nick and Angelo promptly make assholes out of themselves, waving at her with big grins on their faces and acting like the teenagers they haven't been for years. Granted, it's been way less time for Nick than Angelo since he's at least ten years older than me and Nick's barely twenty-five, but they're only embarrassing themselves.

I turn my head to see if she matches the descriptions they've been giving all week, but she must've walked into the back because the only one I see is Meg. She's been here for longer than I can even remember. I know she finds my guys amusing since she's shaking her head and chuckling, but the new girl is nowhere to be found.

The conversation at the table captures my attention and I look away from Meg to see Angelo patting Nick on the shoulder consolingly. "You're much too young my friend," he explains. "A woman like that wants a man who can take care of her and keep her satisfied, not a pup she'll have to train." All five men at the table burst into laughter, though I'm not sure if it's at Angelo's words or the indignant look on Nick's face. Since I'm the boss, I look down at my menu and try to keep the smile off my face.

"Bullshit, old man." Nick raises his arm and flexes it, showing off the muscles he works very hard for. "I can satisfy any woman. All they have to do is look at me and they cream their panties."

This time even I can't stop my laughter. "Boy, if you think that's all it takes, I feel sorry for every woman you've had in your bed."

"Yeah," Simon agrees, "just so you know, those moans in porn? They're *fake*, and so are all the ones you've been hearing."

Everyone starts giving Nick shit after that. It's a good thing the restaurant is pretty empty right now. The benefit of going to lunch after two, I guess.

The soft sound of a throat clearing silences the laughter immediately, and a hard pang goes through my chest when I meet warm brown eyes in a pale, pink-cheeked face. She's even *better* than advertised. I can see why my guys have been making bets on who will get her number first. The second I see her, I want to tell them all to back the fuck off, but I know I can't.

"What can I get for you guys today?"

Boy, if that isn't a loaded question. Directing a glare around the table, I tell them all silently to behave. There's a chorus of, "Hey Hailey" or "Hi darlin'" from the guys sitting at the table as they all start telling her what they want, flirting all the while and making the red in her cheeks deepen.

Hailey. I'm not sure how I haven't heard her name all week, but I don't recall any of the guys ever mentioning it.

I'm the last person to order, and when our eyes meet once again my thoughts scatter. She's staring down at me expectantly, and I can't think straight. She waits patiently, but the longer it takes me to answer, the more unsure she looks. Her brows furrowing in confusion finally breaks me out of my reverie and I tell her to just, "Surprise me."

This widens her eyes and I can see she's starting to panic. "Sweetheart, I'm easy. Patsy's food is the best around and I've never had anything here I didn't like." Her whole body sags in relief and she nods quickly, looking almost like a bobblehead doll. If she wasn't so damn adorable, I'd laugh. Something tells me that would just fluster her further, so I swallow it down.

Once she's gone, the comments and raucous laughter start right back up, but this time they're directed at me.

"So," Nick starts, "it's like that, huh?" The glacial look I give him should shut him up, but it doesn't. "Hey, look, I don't blame you a bit. I'd tap that ass in a heartbeat--"

Hailey's reappearance at our table with a tray full of drinks cuts off whatever he was going to say. She's giving

Nick an icy look of her own, but she doesn't call him out for talking about her. His shoulders slump in embarrassment anyway, and I have to bite the inside of my cheek to keep from smirking smugly at his discomfort.

The second she places the last cup on the table, she spins around and walks away quickly, her spine rigid and I don't know how, but I *know* she's upset.

Nick curses under his breath, but I ignore him. I have no idea what I'm going to say to her, but it doesn't stop me from getting up and going after her anyway.

CHAPTER 2

Hailey

*M*y cheeks are burning as I walk away from their table. Those guys have come in every day this week so far, and yeah, they're always rowdy, but this is the first time they've talked about *me*. Nick seemed like such a sweetheart with the way he's been flirting with me all week, but the comments he was making to the new guy at the table...*oh my God*. I'm so embarrassed.

I drop my empty tray on the counter and tell Meg I'll be right back. She gives me a sympathetic look and nods, thankfully not saying anything. She knows all about what I've been going through, and right now I'm going to use that sympathy to my advantage.

Pushing through the back door, I walk out into the alley and lean against the wall. I shut my eyes and try to calm my heart. It feels like it's about to beat out of my chest.

"I'm sorry." It's *him*. His voice sends a shiver down my spine and goosebumps pop up on my arms. It's deep and sexy, everything a man's voice should be.

The heat of his body caresses my own and my eyes snap open. He's standing right in front of me, *way* too close, but I don't tell him to back up.

"I'm sorry," he says again, remorse filling his eyes as he studies my face.

Clearing my throat, I tell him, "I heard you the first time."

"Well, you didn't say anything."

I straighten, standing to my full height, which is still at least five inches shorter than him. I'm a tall girl, so five inches taller than my five-foot-eight makes him at least an inch or two over six feet. "I wasn't aware it required a response." I know I sound catty, but I can't quite bring myself to care. He *should* be sorry. Actually, *Nick* should be the one out here apologizing for being an idiot, not him.

His lips tip up on one side, totally unaffected by my attitude. Maybe even amused by it. "I guess it didn't, but that doesn't stop me from wanting one anyway."

He takes a step closer to me and I can smell a hint of his cologne, along with motor oil and grease. It shouldn't be an attractive smell, but it is. Before I realize I'm doing it, I take a step back in reaction, putting my back up against the wall again with nowhere to go. If he gets any closer, we'll be touching from chest to groin.

Thinking the word makes me blush harder, but I also look down at the crotch of his jeans for just a second before his chuckle has my eyes flying back up to his face. Humor fills his gaze, but it doesn't stop my mortification, and for the second or third time, my cheeks turn bright red.

Why do I keep embarrassing the hell out of myself in front of this man? What is it about him that makes me turn into an idiot?

We stand here for longer than I'd like to admit staring into each other's eyes. I feel my body start to drift towards his, his doing the same, but then he closes his eyes. Remorse fills his features for barely a second, and when he opens them again, he steps away quickly.

"I'm sorry, I shouldn't be here."

It's his third apology in only a few minutes, but the rest of what he said confuses the hell out of me. He shouldn't be here? *Why not?* And why do I care?

He spins around, and he's gone before I can ask any of the questions filling my head. Even worse, when I go back in, his seat is empty.

"He asked me to box his order for one of the other guys to bring to him." Meg's voice makes me jump, and when I turn to face her, she shrugs. "Whatever happened out there, you freaked Mitchell the hell out." Narrowing her eyes, she tilts her head and considers me. "Be careful with him, Hailey."

Well, that's not cryptic at all.

7

CHAPTER 3

Mitchell

*S*itting in my office I watch through the large window as my crew works on different vehicles. I've spent so much of my life in this office, first as a boy when my grandpa and then my dad ran the garage, then as a teenager and young man learning how they ran the place so I could eventually take over.

Anderson Automotive Repair has become my home away from home, my escape from a reality I no longer want to live. If I thought I could set up a bed in here without getting weird looks, I'd probably do it. That's not true. If I did that, I'd have to explain *why* I was doing it to my kids and that would just make life at home more intolerable.

It's been two days and I'm *still* trying to get Hailey off my mind. I haven't been successful, but I have managed to keep from going back to the restaurant to see her. Don't get me wrong, I want to, I just know it would be wrong. Fucked up in more ways than one. Doesn't mean I haven't spent every spare moment wondering where she is and what she's doing.

Rex, my second-in-command and best friend since we were five comes into the room, shutting the door quietly behind him. There's a look on his face that can be best described as uncertain, and it makes my whole body tense in preparation. All I can do is hope Drew, our newest employee, didn't hurt himself or someone else doing something stupid. It wouldn't be the first time, though last time, it was the windshield of a car that took the most damage.

Please don't make me have to explain to some little old lady why her oil change that should have only taken an hour is going to end up taking two or three days because I have to order replacement parts due to his idiocy.

"What's up?" Rex grimaces, his eyes looking everywhere but at me. "Come on man, you're starting to freak me out."

Shoulders slumping slightly, he sighs. "Okay, look, I don't know why I'm telling you because it shouldn't even matter." Rex pauses like he's trying to gather his thoughts. Either that, or he *really* doesn't want to say whatever it is he's about to.

"Just spit it out. Get it over with so we can decide how to move on, where to go from here."

The laugh that comes out of him is humorless. "Yeah, okay. Sure. Why not?" He takes the seat in front of my desk and bends forward, propping his elbows on his knees and running his hands through his hair before looking back up at me. "Just... don't kill the messenger, alright?"

"For fuck's sake. Tell me, damn it."

"Okay, okay. So, the girl from Patsy's? Hailey?" He winces when he says her name, but that might be because I flinch.

"What about her?"

Rex looks down, unable to meet my eyes for whatever he's about to say. "Nick was talking to her today at lunch. By talking, I mean flirting." I can't even attempt to hold back the growl in my throat. "I guess she mentioned having a problem with her car, so he told her to bring it here after her shift and we would look at it, see what's wrong."

My hands squeeze the edge of my desk so hard I wouldn't be at all surprised to hear the metal squeak, but thankfully, it doesn't. I have to play it cool. There's no other choice. Yeah, Rex knows how crappy shit is at home, but he still wouldn't approve of the instant attraction I have for this Hailey woman. No one would.

"If we have the time, and an empty bay, that should be fine. As long as it doesn't take away from the Miller's car. He's supposed to finish that up by tomorrow. The insurance guy is going to be here at three to do his final inspection. I'm sure Sam and Amelia are ready to turn in that rental and get their car back. Plus, I'm sure Sam is ready not to have the reminder *he* was the one to hit the deer instead of his wife. She said when she came to meet the adjuster that he was always telling *her* to be careful."

Looking at me with his mouth hanging slightly open,

Rex seems speechless. It's probably because that's the most I've talked in one go in at least a year, maybe two. Ever since shit with Tabitha started going downhill, so did my talking.

We don't get the chance to continue. Movement outside my window grabs my attention, and when I turn to face it, I see *her* walking beside Nick. She's grinning up at him, her eyes riveted on him, and I almost lose my mind. Ignoring whatever Rex is surely about to say, I'm out of my chair and striding across the room to my door, the only thing I'm able to focus on getting to her before Nick makes more of an impression.

What the fuck is wrong with me?

CHAPTER 4

Hailey

*C*oming here shouldn't make me nervous, but it does. Actually, after the weird episode with Mitchell the other day, it's probably not such a shock that I'm nervous coming here. Obviously, I did something to cause his insane reaction. It's not often that a man basically runs away from you, but here we are.

I practically sigh in relief when I see Nick standing at the edge of the building talking to one of the other guys wearing a pair of coveralls with "Anderson Automotive Repair" on the back. One thing that's good about those things--they have their names on the front, just above their hearts. Makes remembering their names when they come in for lunch easy.

As soon as he sees me, Nick's face lights up. It makes me feel guilty, like I'm taking advantage of him somehow.

He's a nice guy, and with the amount of flirting he's done with every visit to Patsy's, he seems to be into me. Unfortunately, I don't think he's a day over twenty-five, while I'm...not. At thirty-two, I'm much closer to thirty-five than I am twenty-five, and dating a younger guy doesn't appeal to me *at all*. I already have one toddler, thanks.

He jogs up to greet me like a happy puppy. If he had a tail, the thing would be wagging so hard his butt would be moving with it. The thought has me pulling in my lips to stifle my laughter, but I return his exuberant, "Hey," with a more subdued version of my own.

"So, what exactly is the car doing?"

I wish he hadn't asked me that again. He asked me at the diner, but I didn't know how to explain it there either. "I'm not sure," I tell him with a shrug. "It kinda shakes when I go faster, and sometimes I swear I can hear a tick when the car is running but the radio isn't on." That's something doesn't happen very often because I *love* listening to music, and so does Connor.

Nick nods. "Okay. The shaking thing can be a fairly easy fix. It could just be an issue with your tires not being balanced. The ticking is a little trickier, but we'll take a look." He looks at me expectantly, but I don't know what he wants. Finally, a smile tips up one side of his mouth and he holds out his hand. "I need your keys so I can pull it in." I hand them over, and he looks pointedly across the room. "The waiting room is right over there. I'll try not to take too long."

"That would be great," I assure him with a smile of my own. I need to go get Connor, not that I'm about to tell him about it if I have to.

13

I'm almost to the waiting area when I feel it. The small hairs on the back of my neck stand on end and it feels like a heavy gaze is locked on my back. It's *him*. I don't know *how* I know, but I do.

Turning in a small circle, I try to find him, but I don't see him anywhere in the small room. That's explained when the waiting room door opens to reveal him standing in the doorway. His shoulders are so broad, they take up the whole space. I wouldn't be surprised if he had to turn sideways just to enter.

The thought makes me snicker, and his eyes lock on my smiling lips.

Oh damn.

I *like* having his eyes on me. How stupid is that? After everything Seth put me through, I should be off men for the rest of my life. Instead, all it took was a few hot looks from this man and a couple of minutes smelling his after-shave to have my stomach in knots and my knees weak.

Down Hailey.

"Uh, hey." I groan inwardly at how idiotic I sound. He's staring at me like he's not sure if he hates me or wants to drag my panties down with his *teeth* and all I can say is hey?

Whoa. Wait a minute. Where the *hell* did that thought come from? Clearly, I've been reading too many romance novels.

Mitchell steps aside so I can enter the room, and I hold my breath as I walk past. He's not giving me much room, and I'm afraid if I breathe at all my body will brush against his and I'll spontaneously combust.

CHAPTER 5

Mitchell

*H*ow is it possible she smells *so fucking good* after working at a diner that serves almost all fried food? If the world was fair, she'd smell like onion rings and fish sticks instead of flowery and fresh. Also, where the hell did "onion rings and fish sticks" come from? That's probably the *worst* combination I could have come up with.

As soon as she's through, I let go of the door and let it whisper shut, glad I sprang for that option when we redid the space. The door slamming constantly all day long about did my head in. It's much better now that it slowly shuts, even when client's kids are running back and forth in and out of it.

Hailey whirls around to face me when the door closes in place. "What are you doing in here?"

I'm not sure how to answer her question. Do I go with the truth outright? Or some version of it? I don't want to lie completely, but how do I say, "I can't stay away from you?"

Her quiet gasp tells me I just did. *Fuck me.*

"Why not?"

Her voice quavers when she asks the question, and I can't help but meet her fearful gaze. That pang in my chest goes through me again at the sight. I don't want her to be *scared* of me. I know I haven't been the most stable individual around her, but I'm not a psycho. Running a hand through my unruly hair, I try to think of a way to explain the thoughts bouncing around like pinballs in my head.

Her beauty is distracting though. The glossy deep brown hair she had in a ponytail when I first saw her is down today, waves curling over her shoulders and covering breasts I have no business noticing, but I do. I can't help it. Even under her Patsy's t-shirt, I can tell they're perfect handfuls. The deep purple shirt brings out the brown in her eyes and highlights the pink deepening on her cheeks the longer I stare at her.

It's just fitted enough to show off her tiny waist and tucked into shorts that hit way too high on her toned thighs. She's tall, and with those short little shorts, her legs look like they go on forever.

Hailey quickly grows uncomfortable with my scrutiny and crosses her arms over her chest in an attempt to shield herself. It breaks my concentration, and I'm glad my beard covers the heat I can feel rising in my face.

"Mitchell?"

I have to clear my throat to answer. "Yeah?"

"Why did you leave the other day? One second you were there, but then you were just...gone. Did I do something wrong?"

Her voice sounds unsure, and I know she's regretting the question as soon as it's out of her mouth, so I rush to reassure her. "No sweetheart. You didn't do anything."

"Then...why?"

Lifting my eyes to the ceiling, I wish for an answer to come to me that I can actually tell her. Of course, nothing comes, so I'm left to muddle through on my own. If I tell her the real reason, she's going to hate me. Hell, I *already* hate myself for the thoughts I'm having about her. Maybe *her* hating me would be a good thing.

Fuck it. I'm just going to tell her.

"Because if I'd stayed there alone with you any longer, I would've kissed you."

Her eyes are almost comically wide at my confession. "Would that be such a bad thing?"

I laugh, though there's no humor in it. "Yeah sweetheart, that would be a bad thing." She's about to ask me why, so I say the words I know are going to end anything this could ever be in the future. "I can't, under any circumstances, kiss you. I'm married."

CHAPTER 6

Hailey

"'m married."

His words shatter my poor, barely held together heart. And why? I've only talked to this man *twice*. He shouldn't be able to bring forth any kind of emotion in me, let alone have me feeling like my heart is breaking all over again. I barely got it put back together after what Seth did to it.

"*Married?*" The word comes out as a shriek, and he winces. "If you're married, why would you even *think* about kissing me? You shouldn't be thinking about kissing *anyone*!" My voice just keeps getting louder and louder with each word, but I can't stop it.

Mitchell takes a step forward, reaching out a hand cautiously like he's trying to soothe a wounded animal, and I scramble away from him. I don't stop moving until once again I'm up against the wall and can't go any further.

He doesn't stop coming until he's standing directly in front of me, much like the position we were in yesterday in the alley. His hand comes to rest on the exposed brick beside my head and he leans in, eyes never leaving mine.

"Let me explain."

I scoff. "There's nothing you could say that would make any of this better. We shouldn't even be in this room alone together. God knows what the guys out there think we're in here doing." Freezing as another awful thought comes into my head, I gasp. "Oh my God. Is this something you do a lot?"

His eyes narrow on me and his lips turn down into a dark scowl. "Do *what* exactly? What are you accusing me of?"

"Accusing you of? Oh, that's rich. You know what I'm asking. Do you often corner women in alleys and closed off rooms while your poor wife sits at home thinking you're this good, faithful husband?"

The snarl that comes out of his mouth has me shrinking back into the wall. He leans even further forward though, not giving me even an inch of space. Our noses are only a centimeter apart and I can feel his breath on my face when he speaks.

"Wow. Quick to judge, aren't you? You don't know *anything* about my so-called 'poor wife' but let me clue you in. She's not my *poor* anything. In fact, she's been making my life miserable for the past two years. Hell, much longer than that if I'm being honest."

I start to ask him what he means, but the anger

sparking out of his dark blue eyes keeps me silent. Thankfully, he continues without my having to ask.

"Tabitha's family owns a very successful bank. Much like this garage, it's been passed down from generation to generation and she's lived a very comfortable life. Unfortunately, even though I own this place free and clear, I can't keep her in the manner she's become accustomed to, and she never lets me forget it."

Oh no.

The sympathy on my face must be clear because he looks even more pissed off when he sees it. "Yeah, Hailey. It's rough not being able to give your wife all the crap she thinks she needs to have. And when I can't? She runs crying to Daddy who gladly gives it to her. I tried to put up with it, to just deal, but it kept getting worse and worse. A year ago, I finally told her I was done. I was leaving and wanted a divorce. Know what she said? If I left, she'd disappear with my kids. Obviously, I can't leave Seattle. This company is all I have and people depend on me. Would she really leave? Probably not. But, how do I take that chance? How do I risk losing my kids?"

He sounds so damn sad, so lost, and not able to see she's manipulating him. Or, maybe he does and just doesn't know how to stop her. At this moment, I *hate* his wife. I hate this woman I've never seen.

"Mitchell, I'm sure she wouldn't leave. If her family has owned that bank forever, her whole life is here. If she's so tied to material things, she's not going to want to leave and have to start all over. Surely you can see that, right? Call her bluff. I know it's hard, but a judge isn't going to just let her take your kids and disappear." My voice is rising again because I'm so angry for him.

He shrugs. "I don't want to take the chance. I don't want to break up my family. Isn't it better to stay until they turn eighteen instead of only seeing them every other fucking weekend?"

I can tell the emotion is getting to him too. "No, it's not. All you're doing is showing them that they should stay somewhere toxic. That they should stay somewhere and be miserable."

His eyes slam shut, but not before I see the pain in them. I'm about to say screw it and kiss him anyway, even though it makes me a homewrecking bitch, but before I can, the door opens to reveal a tall, svelte blonde who looks *pissed*.

Her eyes focus on me and I'm glad looks can't kill because I'd be dead.

"What are you doing with my husband?"

Oh shit…

"Tabitha," Mitchell groans, turning so he's standing in front of me and blocking me from her view.

Unfortunately, I can still see her and she is *pissed*. I'm kinda glad Mitchell is between us because the angry energy she is giving off makes me think that if she could get to me, there would be a catfight happening right about now.

She crosses her arms over her ample chest and glares daggers at both of us. "I cannot believe you, Mitchell. How *dare* you do this to me." Tears glisten in her eyes and I watch wide-eyed as one drips down her cheek. For someone as hateful as he insists she is, she just looks like a heartbroken wife who just found her husband about to kiss a woman who is definitely *not* her.

"Stop." She flinches at the venom in his voice and my body goes rigid. He doesn't sound anything like the man who was speaking to me earlier. "Please don't act like you give a shit what I'm doing or who I'm doing it with. We both know we're only married in name only and if I had my choice that wouldn't be the case."

Her head turns to the side like he just smacked her across the face and the pain is clear for anyone to see. "Mitchell…" I whisper his name and his body jerks like he forgot I was here. From what he told me, their relationship is far from good, but that doesn't give him the right to talk to her that way.

"You're such a bastard," she says angrily, though I can hear the tears in her voice. "And you," her focus turns from him to me and I want to hide at the madness I see in her gaze, "you're no better than he is. What type of woman chases a married man?"

Whoa. That's not at all what happened. Mitchell raises his voice again, yelling at her, but her words cut me so deep I can't focus on whatever it is he's saying. She's right. Granted, I didn't know he was married when I first met him, but I was entertaining kissing him after he told me.

"I'm sorry." Now my voice is the one trembling with tears, but all my anger is directed inward.

Stumbling back, the only thing on my mind suddenly is the need to get away from this situation. I don't want any part of this fight that should be between them. I shouldn't have been part of this marriage at all.

"Hailey, stop." The snap of his voice grabs my attention, and before I can think about it, I do exactly what he says and it only makes me hate myself more. I'm shaking my head instinctively as he turns to face me, putting *her* behind him now.

Mitchell's holding his hands up in front of himself and when I look at his face I can see the remorse and apology radiating from him. That's when I realize I'm repeating "I'm sorry, I'm so sorry" over and over again.

I don't want him to touch me because if he does I know I'll fold, I'll do whatever he says and then I'll be right back in the middle of an argument that shouldn't involve me at all.

The moment the path to the door is clear I make a break for it, ignoring the fact that he's yelling my name and that my car is being worked on right now so I don't even have a ride away from here.

I'm counting on his wife keeping him in the little room away from nosy people, and I'm so busy running through the building I don't pay any attention to the concerned eyes on me until I run straight into a chest I don't recognize.

"Hailey?" The voice is familiar, and I'm thankful it is because there are so many tears running down my face right now I can barely see. "Are you okay?"

My head shakes as I sob, unable to put my jumbled thoughts into words at first. Strong hands grab my biceps and pull me into a hug, holding me until my cries quiet long enough to get out the words, "I need to get out of here."

Nick looks down at me, scanning my eyes with his own and trying to figure out what's wrong with me. I can't hold his gaze for long, I'm too embarrassed. "Okay. Let me take you home. Your car won't be done for another hour or so."

I practically sag into him in relief. "Please. I can send someone back for my car later."

Nick leads me out to his car and once we're headed away from the garage I breathe a sigh of relief. I can't decide if I'm sad or mad or what. My body just feels drained from my tears at this point and I can barely focus.

He drops me off at my parents, promising to let me know when my car is ready so I can have someone come get it and I thank every entity I can think of when I walk inside to a quiet and empty house. Mom has taken Connor to the park, so I'm free to go to my room and fall face down onto the bed. I use the alone time to finish crying out all my anger, frustration, and guilt into my pillow until I fall asleep.

CHAPTER 7

Mitchell

$\mathcal{H}$ ailey runs out of the waiting room and I want so badly to chase after her and force her to let me explain. First, I have to deal with Tabitha who's staring at me with a triumphant and smug smile on her face.

"What the hell is wrong with you?"

The question is out before I can contain it and all she does is shrug nonchalantly like she doesn't have a care in the world. "I don't know what you're talking about." She's trying to sound innocent, a play she's made so many times with me I'm immune to it. I used to think I was crazy when I'd accuse her of doing something, but I've learned now that she'll do whatever she can to make herself seem like the injured party.

"Don't." My voice sounds like I'm speaking from deep in my throat when I ground out the word. "Don't even act like you're the injured party here. Why do you even care if I was in here with another woman? We are married in name only, Tabitha. We haven't been anything more than glorified roommates for two years now."

Finally, she drops the act to glare at me. "Mitchell, I don't give a damn what you do or who you do it with, but I'll be damned if you're going to make a fool out of me. Do you know how eager those idiots out there were to tell me you had another woman in here? I'm not going to stand for that."

Ah, so that's what this is about. Her ego. "First, the guys who work for me are *not* idiots. Second, you are seriously going to stand here and tell me that you instigated this whole scene just to save face and make yourself feel better?"

I wish I could say I'm shocked or that I can't believe she'd do that, but I'm not. Not even a little. This is exactly why our marriage hasn't worked for so long. Tabitha is way more concerned about public perception than she is about me or us.

"What did you expect would happen if you flaunted some slut in my face?"

Her words have me seeing red. I stalk forward, forcing her backward until her back hits the concrete wall and am way too satisfied by the fear that fills her eyes. *Good*. She should be scared of me right now.

"Do not *ever* call any woman I'm with a slut, but especially not Hailey. She doesn't deserve that from you or anyone else." My words have Tabitha glaring up at me again, but her glare is nowhere near as powerful as it was a few minutes ago. The difference now is I have the upper hand and nothing else to lose.

A man with nothing to lose is a dangerous one to fuck with and Tabitha is about to learn that the hard way.

Leaning forward even further into her space, I push until we're almost nose to nose and she starts to tremble as she waits for whatever I'm going to do next. I'm not proud of the fact that I'm enjoying her discomfort and fear, but after everything she's put me through in the past couple of years, I can't help the satisfaction I'm feeling at making her uncomfortable for a change.

Once I'm satisfied I have her full attention, I tell her in a low, serious voice, "I'm officially done."

"Done?" she squeaks. "What do you mean, done?"

She's asking the question, but she knows exactly what I mean. I'll explain it to her though to make sure there is no misunderstanding. "I mean just that. I'm *done*. Done trying to keep you happy, done walking on eggshells to keep you from flying off the handle. Done staying in this relationship that does nothing but make me fucking miserable all the goddamn time."

Saying the words makes me feel like a weight has been lifted off my shoulders. I should have done this a long damn time ago. Hailey was right. Staying in this relationship that makes us both unhappy isn't good for us or Ben and Evie. All it does is show them that it's okay for your partner to treat you like shit and I'm done doing that.

Tabitha sputters, not sure what to say. It's been so long since I've stood up to her because I always try to keep the peace, but I'm done being a fucking pussy.

"B-b-but you *can't*."

She might think that, but she's wrong. "The hell I can't. I've stayed too long already." A thought occurs to me and I ask the one question I've been wanting to ask for two years now. "Why would you even want to stay together, Tab? Neither of us is happy. Don't you want a chance to find someone who will make you happy? We're not good for each other, and staying in this relationship is slowly killing us both." I'm not trying to be nasty. The anger I had towards her is gone, replaced by exhaustion and a desire to be finished with all of this.

Tabitha lifts her chin in a stubborn move I've seen way too often. I know when I see it I'm not going to get an answer, not a real one anyway.

"We could be happy again."

I pull back from her in shock. "No, Tabitha, we can't. Too much has happened for us to go back now." Too many nights where she sat beside me on the couch playing games on her phone and ignoring my existence, too many times when she couldn't do something as simple as stop at the store and pick something up or even be bothered to clean up the kitchen when I went to bed too sick to eat.

I'm tired of being the person to do everything for our family while she did whatever the hell she wanted. I don't expect my wife to do all the cooking and all the cleaning, but damn, I expect us to both do the shit work so we can spend time *enjoying* each other.

Telling her all of this *again* is pointless. She won't ever admit to any wrongdoing and if I try to explain she'll just accuse me of attacking her.

I take another step back, and another, putting enough

space between us there's no danger of touching. I've touched Tabitha for the last time.

The only thing I have left to say to her is, "And as far as the kids go, if you try to leave with them, I'll fight you every motherfucking step of the way. You can't hold them over my head anymore. We all deserve more than this."

After delivering my parting shot, I walk calmly out of the waiting room and am almost blindsided by Nick's fist.

"What the hell did you do to her?" He shouts in my face and I snap.

All the rage I have pent up from the past two years explodes on him and I grab him by the neck of his shirt and shove him away from me before stalking after him.

"Where is she?"

Nick laughs. "Where do you think? She left, asshole. I don't blame her either. What kind of asshole brings her into a closed-off room knowing his wife could show up at any moment? Why the fuck would you put her in that position."

Now it's Nick I'm pushing against the wall and getting far too close to in an attempt to make my point known. "Do *not* fuck with me right now, Nicholas. I don't you an explanation, so I'm not telling you shit. What happened is between me and Hailey, so keep your ass out of it. I'll tell her, and *only* her, what she needs to know.

"Good luck with that. You forget, Mitch, I *saw* how upset she was. I'm the one who took her home and watched as she cried. That girl was *devastated* by whatever shit you and the cold bitch perpetrated in that room and I'm not about to help you find her."

I can see the resolve on his face, and as much as I'd like

to beat the information out of him, I know better than to try. It's hard, but I back off, glaring at him the entire time, then turn my back and walk away, barely managing to keep my rage in check. Beating my fist into his face would be counterproductive, and punching the wall will only hurt my hand.

Instead of heading for my office, I go straight to the front desk and pull her phone number off the forms she had to fill out before dropping her car off with us. See, I didn't need Nick after all. Her address would've been better, but beggars can't be choosers.

Putting the phone to my ear, I listen to it ring before her voice hits my ears. I clench it tighter in my hand and struggle for what to say. She says hello a second time, but all I can do is say her name.

She gasps in my ear. "You have some nerve calling me, Mitchell."

"Please, Hailey, you have to let me explain what that was."

The line is silent for so long I pull the phone away to make sure it's still connected, then she says, "I don't have to *let* you do anything. I have zero interest in being the third person in your relationship. My ex already did that to me once. I refuse to live through it again in the other position."

My free hand fists at my side. "That's not going to happen."

"You're right," her voice says quietly, sadness clear even through the phone line. "Goodbye, Mitchell. Don't call me again. This number and any others you call from will immediately be blocked."

With those words, the connection between us ends and even though she said she was blocking me, I still try to call her, staring down at the screen in disbelief when I get the "your call can't be completed" message.

Rage fills me once more and I throw the stupid thing at the wall, watching it shatter and fall to the floor.

CHAPTER 8

One year later

Hailey

*I*t's almost time for the parents to start coming in so I can meet them and the children who will be my charges for the school year starting in a little over a week. I take a few deep breaths, trying to calm myself down so I don't look like a crazy woman when they walk through the doors.

While I wait, I look around the room at all the posters I spent hours picking out and hanging up, as well as the neat rows of desks and brightly colored paper stacked on top of them, makes me giddy. Being a teacher is all I wanted to do from the time I was a little girl, and the fact that I'm *finally* living my dream has my chest feeling like it's about to burst with happiness.

Sure enough, the first set of parents walks through the open door and it's hard to stay standing beside my desk. The principal, Mrs. Sanders, warned me and the two other teachers who are new to the school this year not to seem too eager. She said if we were, the parents would think they could walk all over us. I don't want to give that impression.

The little girl makes a beeline for the reading corner I've set up in one corner of the room. Grabbing a book out of one of the bins, she immediately plops down to make herself comfortable in one of the three bean bag chairs and starts flipping through the pages. I already know we're going to get along well because if given the choice, I'm going to be reading instead of talking to grown-ups too.

Turning my attention back to her parents, I decide, screw the principal's advice. I don't want to come off like I'm one of the stuck-up teachers I loathed when I was in school. I want to build happy, trusting relationships with the parents of my students.

Decision made, I walk over to meet them, holding out a hand for them to shake. "Hi! I'm Hailey Lucas and I'll be your daughter's teacher this year."

The excitement in my voice is clear, making both parents relax as they return my smile and take my proffered hand, first the father, then the mother, before introducing themselves as well. "I'm Stacey Montgomery, and this is my husband Isaac." The pretty redhead turns slightly to focus on her daughter. "The little bookworm over there is Sophie."

"She gets that from her mother," Isaac shares, his warm

brown eyes sparkling with a joke only he and his wife understand.

Leaning further into him, she explains, "I review books, so I'm always reading something."

"Oh, I bet that's a fun job." It's true. Normally, when I think of book reviewers, I think of stuffy old men publishing scathing reviews in the paper, not someone like Stacey Montgomery who's beautiful and friendly, her smile and personality drawing people in.

Realizing I've been staring at her much too long while I think about the differences between her and the reviewers I'm used to hearing about, I turn my attention to her husband. "And what do you do, Mr. Montgomery?"

"Please, call me Isaac," he says with a grin and a wink that makes his wife roll her eyes in a way that says she deals with his charm often. "I own a construction company."

His profession isn't shocking at all. He's tall and lean, but his arms and shoulders clearly say he does plenty of physical labor.

Get a grip, Hailey. He's the *father* of one of your *students.* It's been way too long since I've been around someone as attractive as he is. The thought makes me think of Mitchell, the asshole I met a few months ago who was also too attractive for his own good... and married just like Isaac.

Ugh. He has no business invading my thoughts. I've been working so hard to forget I ever met him, but I'm failing.

Forcing myself to focus back on the conversation I've

been having with the Montgomerys, I pretend not to notice the concerned looks they're both giving me and paste a smile on my face. "I'm sure I can count on you coming in for career day, right? The kids love hearing about putting things together and tearing them apart almost as much as they love doing it themselves."

Isaac chuckles but assures me he will, and I spend a few more minutes explaining what I'm planning to do this year with their daughter, a speech I've spent the last week and a half preparing and memorizing since I know I'll be saying so many times.

More families are coming in, so I let the Montgomerys go explore the room and what I'm planning to have their daughter study this year while I go greet the others. Meeting all the kids I'm going to be teaching this year makes that exploding feeling in my chest bigger, and I feel like I'm where I'm supposed to be…finally.

The meet the teacher time is almost over when the hair on the back of my neck stands on end. Praying to every deity I know, I turn around slowly, hoping it's not who I think it is, but my wishes go unanswered.

Standing in the doorway is Mitchell in all his bearded and tattooed glory. Any hope I had that my memory of him was exaggerated dies as we stare at each other in disbelief. Surely fate wouldn't be so cruel as to have his child in my class.

Please, please let him just be in the wrong room.

That request goes unanswered too when the adorable dark-haired girl at his side says in a sweet little voice, "Are you Ms. Lucas?"

I can't ignore her. Crouching down so we're eye-level, I confirm, "I am Ms. Lucas. Who are you?"

She ducks her head and leans heavily into the man I'm trying desperately to ignore. I almost look up at him, wanting to share with him how precious she is, but stop myself at the last second. He's the enemy, even if his daughter is in my class and I'm not going to make any of this easy for him.

After a few seconds of hiding, Mitchell reaches down to cup her shoulder with his big hand and she lifts her gaze to his. "Tell her your name, honey."

That voice… saying that endearment… I'm fairly sure my ovaries just exploded. I have *got* to get a handle on my hormones.

His daughter finally peers up at me and takes a deep breath. "Evie."

I think back on my student list, but I don't remember seeing an Evie on it. Relief courses through me, but Mitchell's next words obliterate it.

"Evelyn," he says, and without thought, I look up at him and freeze.

He's staring down at where I'm practically on my knees in front of him and his blue eyes are so dark they're almost black. His free hand is fisted at his side and the sight of him starts my heart racing. "What?"

"Her name. It's Evelyn Anderson, but she prefers Evie." Mitchell says this like he's extremely disgruntled about this fact, which only makes me determined to only call her Evie just to irritate him.

Turning my attention back to her, I hold out a hand.

"Evie, would you like to see your classroom?" She nods, looking up at me shyly when I stand to my full five-foot-eight and grabs my hand, a toothy smile gracing her pretty face when she sees her name written on a wide white strip covered in butterflies.

Once I'm finished showing her around the classroom, I take her back to where her dad is still standing, eyes on both of us. I've been able to feel his stare the whole time and it's done nothing but make me nervous.

"We need to talk." He leans in close to say the words in a voice low enough no one else can overhear. I can smell his unique blend of car and cologne, and the scent has me closing my eyes and breathing deeply to savor it before I realize what I'm doing.

I know better than this, I swear I do.

My body sways closer to his without my permission, but then I hear Evie's voice calling for her mom and feel his body stiffen at the same moment mine goes rigid. It takes everything in me to take a step back from the warmth of his body, but I manage... barely.

"No, Mitchell. We don't have anything to say to each other."

He looks like he wants nothing more than to argue, but Evie's voice is getting closer and the last thing I want is another confrontation with his wife. The last one was more than enough.

Mitchell looks over his shoulder, and I guess he has the same thought I do because he backs off. "This isn't the time, but we *are* going to talk, Hailey. A lot has changed since I saw you last."

With that ominous statement, he leaves my classroom and I shut the door before anyone else comes down the hall. A quick look at my watch reveals the meet and greet is just about over and I slowly sink to the floor in relief.

How am I supposed to do this? How can I be his daughter's teacher and still keep my distance from him? I don't know what it is about him, but staying away is a struggle. It shouldn't be, considering he's *married* and I'm not that type of woman, but it's like my body, maybe even my *soul* is drawn to him whenever he's near.

I can't go to the principal and ask her to remove Evelyn from my class either. That will just give him the irrefutable proof he affects me and I don't want to give him that kind of power over me. No, I'm stuck. I'll just have to do whatever I can to keep my walls up around him and not let him get to me.

Easier said than done.

The bell rings, signaling the end of the evening and I rush to get my stuff together so I can go home and cuddle with my son. There are still a few days before school starts, so I'm going to take advantage of this time with him before he goes back to daycare. And use the time to build up any defense I can against Mitchell Anderson.

When I walk out into the parking lot, he's far enough ahead of me I can study him without him seeing me. Strangely, it's just him and his daughter, along with a boy who must be his son. *Where did his wife go?* Evelyn, *Evie*, was talking to her in the hallway, but she isn't with them now. Did she go ahead of them to start the car? That doesn't seem right.

Ugh. I have got to get a handle on this. Thinking about

him isn't going to cause me anything but heartache and I *refuse* to do to someone else what Seth did to me. Being the person who's cheated on is the worst, and no matter how hateful she is, his wife deserves better than that... and so do his kids. *So, do I.*

CHAPTER 9

Mitchell

*W*hat the hell are the chances Hailey would be my daughter's teacher? I'm not sure if fate is the best fucking thing ever or if karma is proving just what a bitch she can sometimes be.

Tabitha is in the hall with Ben and Evie, paying more attention to whatever is on her phone screen than what Evie is telling her about her new teacher. That's probably a good thing because if Tabitha knew Hailey was the teacher, she'd probably explode. Tabitha blames Hailey for being the reason I finally decided I was done with her shit and called the bluff of her taking my kids to California if I left.

She's not altogether wrong. Meeting Hailey *was* what finally made me grow a pair and tell her I was done. I knew there was no way Hailey would get involved with me if I was still married and I never would've asked her to do that either.

I reach the three of them just as the door to Hailey's classroom shuts, the sound probably not as loud in reality as it sounds in my head considering there are still kids running up and down the halls and parents discussing their children with the teachers who will be spending all day with them this year.

Personally, I'm grateful Hailey shut the door because if she hadn't, Tabitha might have decided to go in and try to intimidate her the way she always has Ben's teachers in the past. If she had her way, Ben would be the mini version of her entitled asshole brother, and that'll happen over my damn dead body.

It's the beginning of Tabitha's week with the kids, and I'm eager to get the handoff over with so I can go find Hailey and convince her to let me explain.

Evie instantly transfers her attention from her mom to me as soon as I'm within reach, and as much as I'd like to ignore her mother, I try not to be a total dick when they're around. Not that it stops her.

"Mitchell."

Tabitha sneers my name like I've done something terrible to her, and I know it's a way to get me to react. I refuse to give her the fight she's looking to start and just nod my head in acknowledgment before turning my attention to Ben.

"What did you think of your teachers, Ben?"

He looks down at his shoes and shrugs. This is the big downside to the divorce. At thirteen, Ben blames me for his mom being the way she is and she does everything she can to stoke his anger. Unless I want to tell him what a bitch his mom truly is, I'm stuck bearing the brunt of his unhappiness, and unlike Tabitha, I'm not putting either of my kids in the middle of our issues. They were there for way too long already.

Knowing it's pointless to try to get him to say more, I turn my attention to Evie and hug her since I know she'll accept it gladly. At least one of my kids still wants to be around me. "Have fun with your mom this week. I love you." Having our "week" start on Wednesday is a pain in the ass sometimes, but at least we both get equal time with the kids.

My shoulders tense when Tabitha sighs. Before she speaks I know she's about to piss me off and disappoint the kids.

"Actually," she starts, sounding like *I'm* the one changing things at the last minute instead of her. "I need you to keep the kids until Friday."

I love the way she says it like it's no big deal. She doesn't bother to ask if she's inconveniencing me because she doesn't give a shit if she is or not, she never has. Plus, she knows I won't refuse because she'll make it out like I don't *want* Ben and Evie around and that's the opposite of the truth.

"Fine." Part of me wants to ask why, but I know that's what she wants so I refrain. She watches me for a few minutes, eyes narrowing when I don't rise to the bait and I can tell it's killing her that I'm not asking questions.

Telling them goodbye and leaving without looking back is something she's able to do so easily. I don't understand it, but I don't have time right now to think about it either. Now that I have them for an extra two days, I need to get them home and figure out what to feed them.

I keep trying to get Ben to talk about his teachers and the classes he's taking in seventh grade, but all I get from him on the way to my truck is one-word answers. Getting this kid to engage with me is like pulling teeth. Luckily, Evie has no problem telling us both all about "Ms. Lucas" and all the things she's going to do this year.

After making sure both kids are in the truck and buckled, I turn to start the car and freeze when I see her getting into her car. So much for trying to talk to her tonight. She doesn't look at me, but the way her shoulders are hunched slightly forward tells me she can feel my gaze on her. Knowing she's still just as affected by me as I am her makes me grin as I start the truck.

"Daddy, can we have hamburgers for dinner?" Evie isn't asking for burgers made at home. She wants a kids' meal with a toy and crappy drive-through burgers.

It will piss Tabitha off when she finds out, but burgers sound good to me, even if the ones I make on the grill taste ten times better than anything we'll get at a fast food place. Fast food is easy though, and it means I don't have to stop at a grocery store on the way home. "Sure, sweetheart." I don't ask Ben because I know he'll go along with whatever Evie wants, and he won't answer me anyway.

We're just pulling into the parking lot of the apartment I rented after the divorce when I see the same car from the school parking lot. Is she here visiting someone?

My luck fucking sucks. I can't go say anything to her tonight, and I don't know when I'll see her again without my kids.

Mine are racing each other up the stairs, leaving me to carry in all the food when I see her heading up the stairs to the building next to mine holding hands with a boy who looks to be a few years younger than Evie. I can't see him well because both their backs are to me, but her head is turned towards him and the love on her face is clear.

As much as I want to follow her and see where she's going, to force her to talk to me, to hear what I have to say, I don't. I head for my apartment and my kids. Making things clear to Hailey will just have to wait.

CHAPTER 10

Hailey

*W*hen I get to my mom's to pick up Connor, she has dinner ready and waiting for me to eat. I'm not about to complain because after talking to all the parents and kids I am starving and was so not looking forward to having to figure out what to eat that Connor will agree to.

The smell of mom's chicken and rice casserole fills the kitchen and as soon as I smell it my stomach growls like I haven't eaten in a week instead of just a few hours. Mom's standing at the stove when I walk in and she starts to laugh when she hears the noise my belly is making.

"Hungry much?" she asks, turning to face me and holding two plates in her hands.

I reach over and grab them from her. "Definitely. Spending two hours explaining my teaching methods to parents takes a lot of energy." Of course, seeing and trying to avoid the man who makes my body, heart, and brain pull in different directions is probably the real reason my energy level is zero. Mom doesn't need to know that though.

"I'm sure," she agrees just as my dad walks into the room with Connor on his shoulders. "Eric! Put that child down before he smacks his head on the ceiling fan."

Dad chuckles and Connor lets loose a belly laugh. "Like I'd let that happen, right Con?" My son continues to laugh, bending forward with my dad so he can pull him off his shoulders and put him on a chair. At first, he acts like he's going to try to sit him down headfirst which just makes Connor laugh harder.

My heart squeezes at the sight and I wish he had this type of relationship with his dad. Seth hasn't seen him since the day I left. He hasn't even attempted to. If it wasn't for the child support getting deposited every other week I'd wonder if he disappeared off the face of the earth.

Passing me on his way to his chair, dad stops to drop a kiss on the top of my head and wrap an arm around my shoulders to give me a quick hug. "Hey, honey."

Connor doesn't even acknowledge my presence when he sees the plate of food in front of him. He's a picky eater, but the stuff he will eat he scarfs down like he's just as starved as my stomach sounded a few minutes ago.

While we eat, mom asks about the students I'll have in my class this year and I try to keep my explanations vague when I mention Evie. Mom doesn't know about Mitchell or what happened last year. I'm not sure why I didn't tell her, because I usually tell her everything, but I kept all of that drama to myself. She's never going to meet him, so it wouldn't have mattered.

Even my mind doesn't believe me when I say there won't be a meeting between Mitchell and my family. The man needs to get the hell out of my head. I've already spent so many months mourning what wasn't meant to be and I've moved on from thinking about him in any way. Why did he have to show back up *now*?

Thankfully, mom doesn't ask any deep questions about my kids. She's pretty familiar with the school though because she was the librarian there for many years. In fact, she's the reason I got the job teaching there. Mom and the principal are good friends, and I know she hired me as a favor to mom. It got my foot in the door so I'm not complaining. I'm going to do everything I can to show them both hiring me was a good decision.

Once we're finished eating and mom has packed up the leftovers for me to take home it's time for us to go. Connor's bedtime is soon and he still needs a bath and some time to chill out. Plus, I want to spend time with just him. He's been here all day and I'm sure my mom needs a break, even if she'll never say it. She's been a godsend since I moved back, keeping Connor until I could find a daycare I was comfortable leaving him at and letting us stay here much longer than I originally planned.

We've only been in our new apartment for two weeks. I wanted to move into my own place with enough time to get Connor acclimated before the school year started and things change for him again. He doesn't do well with change and he's had so much of it in the past two years.

"Are you sure you don't want to just spend the night here?"

Mom's voice is full of concern and I almost relent just to make her feel better. "No, that's okay. Connor needs to get used to sleeping at our place instead of yours before preschool starts next week." And I need time alone so I can think about ways to avoid the "conversation" Mitchell wants to have. There can't possibly be anything he can say I'll want to hear.

"Okay." Mom doesn't sound very sure about my decision, but that's because she'll always see me as the little girl running after her brother and coming home with her knees all skinned up instead of a woman who knows her own thoughts and feelings.

Connor chatters all the way across town to our apartment and doesn't stop until we're in the living room and he's been told to get his bath stuff together. He loves playing with toys in the tub still, and he knows if he forgets something he'll be out of luck.

I let him spend more time in the bath than I normally would, loving the sound of him enjoying himself, and we watch two episodes of his favorite show before he finally starts yawning and rubbing his sleepy eyes.

The minute he's in bed and asleep I head for the kitchen and pour the biggest glass of wine I can find before opening my phone to my text app and sending a message to my best friend Riley.

Me: You'll never guess who I saw at school tonight

Riley: Who???

Me: Mitchell

Not even five minutes go by before there's a loud

knock on my door. She doesn't stop banging on it until I pull it open and glare. "Are you *trying* to wake up Connor?"

"Sorry." She doesn't sound it all when she breezes past me straight into the kitchen to grab her own full glass of wine. She makes herself comfortable on the couch and waits for me to do the same before she starts her interrogation. "Where did you see him?"

I tell her all about seeing him in my classroom and how I'm going to be teaching his daughter and a big grin lifts her full lips the more I talk. "This is fantastic."

"Out of everything I said, that's all you've got to say? What part of this mess is *fantastic?*" I don't give her the chance to answer before I do it for her. "None of it, that's what."

Riley rolls her eyes. "Bullshit. You've been mooning over this guy for months. I think you should hear what he has to say."

My mouth gapes open with shock. "Seriously? You think I should hear what some guy who almost kissed me while he was *married* has to say? Who are you and what did you do with my best friend?"

I can't believe she thinks I should listen to anything he has to say. Shouldn't my best friend have *my* interests at heart? It seems like she's on his side, and that thought *hurts*.

"You never know," she says with a shrug. "It's been a year, things could've changed a lot since the last time you saw him."

Who cares if they have? "Even if something *has* changed, he's still a cheater."

Now she rolls her eyes. "Hails, is he really? I mean, you didn't *actually* do anything, right? He backed off... and he told you he was married. A scumbag slimeball would have taken advantage of the situation *and* you, but he didn't. Doesn't that at least buy you listening to him say whatever it is he needs to? If nothing else, it will give you some closure."

I glare at her, mad that she's making sense when I wanted her to tell me I'm right and I should ignore him forever if possible. "I don't like you."

"No, you don't like when I'm *right*." My glare deepens, but she just laughs. "Look, I'm just saying, maybe you should talk to him. Let him say whatever it is he wants to say and then make a decision. Maybe after you'll at least be able to teach his kid without wanting to throw up every time you see him."

Ugh. "Damn you and your logic." She doesn't reply, just stares at me with one eyebrow raised and a knowing look in her eyes. "Fine, you win. I'll talk to him, but I don't think it's going to solve anything. Nothing can change the fact that he was married when I first met him, but maybe whatever he has to tell me will make me feel better about everything."

Riley smiles triumphantly and bounces out of her seat with an amount of glee I don't understand, but I don't get to ask because after giving me a quick kiss on the cheek she's gone, leaving me sitting in the living room of my new apartment and contemplating the possibility that maybe I was wrong about Mitchell to begin with... and not in a bad way.

CHAPTER 11

Mitchell

I've tossed and turned all night, so when my alarm goes off I feel like absolute dog shit and all I want is to go back to sleep for eight more hours. Unfortunately, being the boss means I can't do that, so once my mom shows up to stay with kids I head for the shop to get my day started.

I've only been at work an hour when Nick comes into the office with a pissed off look on his face. "There's someone here to see you." The attitude he has about has me intrigued.

"Who is it?"

He just shakes his head and leaves, letting the person walk in as he does and I stare at her in shock. Before she can say anything, I stand and walk around my desk to stand in front of her, almost unable to believe she's standing here.

"Hailey?"

Looking uncomfortable, her eyes dart around my office, focusing on anything but me. I want to grab her and force her to look at me, wanting to see her eyes when she tells me why she's here, and I have to shove my hands in my pockets to keep from doing it.

"Hey," she says softly, tucking her hair behind one ear so it won't fall in her face.

She still hasn't looked at me, so I lean back on my desk, hoping the pose is casual enough to alleviate some of her nervousness. Towering over her definitely isn't going to help.

A few minutes go by and the quietness in the room starts to become stifling. I want to give her whatever time she needs, but I can't stand the awkward silence anymore.

"What are you doing here? Don't get me wrong, I'm happy you're here… I just don't know *why* you're here."

As soon as I say the words I want to kick myself for sounding like a desperate idiot. Why can't I keep my mouth shut around her?

Her voice is barely audible when she replies. "You said you wanted to explain, so I'm here to listen."

I can't disguise my shock. Yesterday she was adamant she wasn't interested in anything I had to say. Now she's here telling me to explain things to her. I guess I shouldn't question it, but I sort of want to. It seems too good to be true.

"Hailey," I say her name, not sure where I want to start. I didn't anticipate having this conversation, and if I'm honest I don't want to have it *here*. This room is so small, and there's an entire building full of my employees on the other side of it. There's almost no privacy either.

"This isn't the right place for this," I finally tell her. She looks up at me questioningly, and I try to explain my reasoning. "I'd rather have this conversation somewhere we have at least a semblance of privacy." Throwing out a hand, I gesture to the room outside my office. "The chances of someone eavesdropping at the door over there are high, and I don't think either of us want that to happen."

She looks shocked like she can't believe she didn't think of that herself, and a blush heats her face. There's no reason for her to be embarrassed, but she doesn't give me the chance to tell her that.

"You're right. Sorry, I-I shouldn't have come."

She turns, fumbling with the closed door and I rush to stop her, putting a hand on the door and holding it closed. My chest is right up against her back and I feel her shiver when we touch. Knowing she's still affected by me has me pressing closer, loving the feel of her against me.

"You absolutely should've come. I just don't want to talk here. Let me take you somewhere." I feel her stiffen, but after a few seconds, her body relaxes and she sighs, nodding her head just enough for me to see her agreement before she drops her hand from the doorknob so I can pull the door open.

I want to put my hand on her back to lead her to my truck, but I'm afraid that might be pushing my luck too far. It's not necessary anyway because she heads straight for my truck, stopping at the passenger side and waiting for me to let her in. I could just beep the locks and let her do it herself, but I'm suddenly desperate for any touch of hers I can get so I reach around her to open the door. It doesn't hurt that it allows me to inhale the scent of her perfume either.

Once we're in my truck, I freeze, not knowing where to take her, but she saves me with an offer. "We can go to my place if you want."

"Sure." She'll probably feel more comfortable there anyway. "How do I get there?"

Hailey starts giving me directions and I realize the stairs she was going up last night must be to *her* apartment, not a friend's. How is it possible we live in the same complex and in all this time I haven't seen her? I should probably tell her I live there too, but I don't. Waiting until after we have our talk would probably be better.

The rest of the trip to her apartment is silent, and the closer we get the more she starts to fidget. I want to reassure her, but I don't know what to say to make her feel better. Thankfully, the trip isn't long, so the silence doesn't last too long, but the moment I put the truck in park she's got the door open and she's jumping down, leaving me to do the same because I'm afraid she's going to run from me. Something spooked her in the ride over and I need to find out what it was.

CHAPTER 12

Hailey

*W*hy did I go to his garage? I feel like an idiot, and the longer I sit here in his truck beside him the worse the feeling becomes. The second he parks, I jerk open the door and jump down, needing to get away from him, from the smell of his cologne that assaulted my senses all the way here. I can't think straight around him.

What was I thinking offering to let him come here? Now he'll know where I live and how to find me. What a dumb idea that was.

I'm so far in my head I don't notice him come over to stand beside me until he takes my hand in his.

"Breathe, Hailey." His voice is pitched low and soothing and I suck in a large breath. *God, why am I acting like this*? I need to chill out. "We don't have to do this if it's too hard. I can wait."

His voice is so gentle, but I can hear the underlying sadness. He wants to explain things to me, and after talking to Riley last night I feel like I owe him the chance to do so. Even if all it does is give me closure so I can move on from thoughts of him. It's been a year since that day in his waiting room, but the pain is just as fresh now as it was then.

I take a moment to gather my courage and straighten my spine. "No, it's fine. Let's get this over with." His flinch is small, but I still see it out of the corner of my eye and instantly want to apologize. I swallow the words. He deserves that and so much more from me.

We walk up the stairs and into my apartment and I watch as he looks around the still bare space. I know what he's seeing, an apartment that looks like it's not even been lived in yet. He's not totally wrong since my brother helped me move in just last weekend. I haven't had a chance to do much of anything, and there are still boxes all over the place.

"Are you moving in or out?" he asks, his amusement clear.

I look away from him before I answer. "I've only been here a week."

He tenses at my admission and I wonder why. What does it matter if I moved in last week or last month or last year? He wasn't with me and we had to get settled eventually. As much as I love my parents, there's no way I could live with them forever.

Leading him over to the small couch that's the only

piece of actual furniture in my living room right now, I gesture for him to take a seat before taking my own at the opposite end. Unfortunately, the couch is small so we aren't very far apart.

Mitchell turns to look at me and I watch the emotions cross his face – indecision, determination, regret. The last is the one that gets me. Having the knowledge he regrets what happened last year makes me feel *so* much better about it.

"What you said last year, about being miserable and what it was teaching my kids, it really fucked me up, Hailey."

The look he gives me tells me just how deep it cut him when I said that. "I refuse to feel bad for that because I still stand by it. It took me a long time to realize I wasn't doing Connor any favors by putting up with Seth's bullshit. We are both so much happier now."

He hurries to reassure me. "You shouldn't feel bad about saying it. It was the kick in the ass I needed to make a change. Well," he stops for a second and looks down at his hands, "that and the way Tabitha acted in the room that day. That was the last straw for me. I knew I had to make a change, and after you left that afternoon I ended it with her for good."

I have so many questions I want to ask him, but when I open my mouth, he holds up one hand and shakes his head. "Let me get this all out. It wasn't like I told her I was leaving and *bam* it was done. She fought every damn step of the way. The thing about Tabitha though, she cares *way* too much about what other people think. Threatening to air all our dirty laundry slowed her down and it let me get everything in place I needed. Now I don't have to worry about her taking off with the kids or telling outrageous lies to hurt me."

"I'm glad, Mitchell." It's true, I'm so glad he's out of that toxic environment, and not only that *he* is, but so are his kids. They're the innocent ones in all of this and they don't deserve to suffer for the choices the two of them make.

He smiles. "Me too." His eyes remain intent on mine, and he slides a little closer to me so he can take one of my hands in his. "You're the reason I was able to see what I was doing was hurting my kids. What you said about me being miserable and teaching my kids to stay in a situation like that opened my eyes."

This time I'm the one looking down at my hands because I said what I did partly for selfish reasons. I'm just glad it worked out for him because it could have gone the opposite way. I almost feel like I should be sorry because he ended a relationship he'd been in for so many years the guilt of knowing that is real.

Mitchell slides a little closer to me and I tense, though I'm not sure exactly what I'm expecting him to do. Maybe it's more what I *want* him to do which is an even scarier thought.

He takes my hands in his and I realize I've been twisting my fingers into knots while sitting here. Knowing he's seeing the sign of my nerves is mortifying, but it's too late to do anything about it.

I keep expecting him to look up at me, but his focus is on my hands. He's stroking the back of them with his thumbs and making goosebumps rise on my arms. That might be worse than him seeing me twist my hands around while listening to him talk.

"Are you happy now? Or, well, I mean, are you *happier* now than you were?" I'm praying he says yes so I won't feel so awful about pushing him to do it.

Now his eyes do come up to meet mine. "I am. It feels like a weight has been taken off my chest, like I can finally breathe again." His focus turns to a spot in my living room so he's not looking at me when he continues. "Having my kids go back and forth between her house and my apartment *sucks*, but it's better than forcing myself to be somewhere I don't want to be with someone who doesn't want me."

I nod, knowing exactly what he means. Our situation isn't exactly the same, but it's close enough. "Yeah, I get that. I didn't want Connor having to grow up without his dad around but doing *everything* by myself while he went out with his friends or did whatever else he was doing when he wasn't at home was way worse. Even living with my parents again was worth it."

Baring my soul to him isn't what I planned on doing this morning, and when I look away from him, my eyes stop on the clock on the wall across from where we're sitting, and I panic.

"Oh crap. I was supposed to meet my mom to get Connor ten minutes ago." We both stand, and while I should apologize for basically kicking him out of my apartment, I'm too busy grabbing my phone and keys so I can get out of here. She's going to ask so many questions about why I'm late and I don't want to answer any of them. Mom has a way of getting things out of me, especially when I don't want to tell her my secrets, so I'm sure she'll have the whole story five minutes after I walk into the house.

Mitchell follows me out the door and down the steps to the parking lot. I look around, searching for my small car, then mentally facepalm myself when I remember we brought his truck here. *Mine* is still at his garage.

God, I'm an idiot.

"C'mon, I'll give you a ride to your car." He's so calm and matter of fact, like the abrupt end to our conversation doesn't faze him at all. It just makes me more anxious because we didn't have any kind of closure. That's the whole reason I went to his office today, and now it's ruined.

We're just leaving the parking lot when he clears his throat, making me jump about two feet in the air. It's so attractive. I don't even blame him for even attempting to hide his chuckle at my discomfort. If it was anyone but me, I'd probably laugh too.

"I want to see you again."

My head spins around so fast when he says this, I probably look like I'm possessed. "What?" is my super intelligent response. Surely, I didn't hear him correctly. I couldn't have.

"I said, I want to see you again." His amusement is so obvious it causes a bright red flush to work its way up my throat to my cheeks.

This entire day has me so confused and turned around. Nothing is happening the way I thought it would. So much for spending half my night going over scenarios about what this conversation would be like. Out of all the options I had planned out in my head, this was *not* one of them.

"Why?"

His laughter fills the cab at my question. "Because, Hailey, I *like* you. You're sweet and you're fun. Even back when I first met you, I was drawn to you. I want to see why."

I don't know how to respond to that. His words warm my heart, and other parts of my body, but my head is not ready to go there with anyone, not yet. It's only been two years since Seth and I split up and the scars from that relationship are still barely scabbed over.

Luckily, I'm saved from having to say anything because we pull into the garage parking lot. Just like when we first pulled up to his apartment, I jump out of his truck and rush to my car as fast as I can without flat out running. If it wasn't for the fact that I am the *most* unattractive runner, I might have attempted it.

Mitchell yells my name from behind me, but I ignore him, slinging open my car door and practically jumping inside. Scaredy cat is a title I will gladly accept. He reaches my door just as I hit the lock button to keep him out and I studiously avoid looking over at him when he tries to talk to me.

After a few seconds, I can hear his sigh. It's so loud it comes through the window. "Okay, Hailey. Have it your way…" I almost relax, but then he says, "for now," right before I pull away from him. My hands are shaking, and when I hit the first red light, I focus on taking deep breaths to steady myself.

Mitchell Anderson is not *what I need right now.*

CHAPTER 13

Mitchell

$\mathcal{I}$'m still thinking about Hailey and the way she ran away from me earlier when I take Evie to dance class. What I said to her shouldn't have been a shock. We were drawn to each other the moment we met. Of course, I'd want to see where that goes.

As much as I'd like to focus my attention on what my next move with her will be, today is important to Evie. This class is a type of showcase, where they'll be showing off one of the dances they'll be doing in their recital next month and debuting the outfits they are planning to have us all purchase for the event. It's my least favorite part of her taking dance because there's constantly an outfit to buy or a competition to pay for and Tabitha hates to spend money on anything but herself.

The minute we walk in the door, Evie takes off for her

group of friends standing on one side of the room. Since she won't remember I'm here until it's time to show off, I head over to where there are a couple of parents I know hanging out together.

"Hey man," Isaac Montgomery greets me when I join them. He's standing in a group that includes his brother Caleb, his brother-in-law Luke and Luke's brother Mark. Mark's married to one of the owners of the studio, who just happens to be who Evie wants to be when she grows up.

I say hi to him and the rest of the group, listening as they continue their discussion about the classes each of their kids are taking and Mark bragging on how good the choreography his wife Meredith came up with is.

There's not much I can contribute, so I just listen to the good-natured ribbing the four of them do, wishing my brother and I had the close relationship they clearly do.

After a few minutes, the conversation turns to the upcoming school year and Caleb asks Isaac about which class his daughter is in. His daughters are teenagers now, but they went to the same school, so he knows a lot of the teachers.

"Sophie's teacher is new this year. She seems nice though, Sophie can't wait until school starts so she can read all the books in her classroom."

Caleb laughs. "Like mother, like daughter. Better watch it, Isaac. Sophie will be stealing those books her mom reads before you know it."

Isaac's face freezes at the thought and I swear I see him shudder. "Jesus, don't put that thought in my head. As far as I know, Sophie's never dating *or* reading those books. Nope, not happening."

All of us laugh because we know he's wrapped around that little girl's finger. He wouldn't tell her no if he found her reading one of her mom's books, he'd probably just buy her some of her own.

Ignoring his brothers, he turns to me and asks what teacher Evie has. "Ms. Lucas." Just saying her name conjures images of her from today. The way she seemed so nervous around me and the way she understood exactly how I felt knowing I needed to be done with my relationship with Tabitha.

"Ms. Lucas, that's right. I couldn't remember her name. Stacey knows it I'm sure, but I'm shit at remembering them. Sophie will be happy they're in the same class again this year. She loves Evie."

"Yeah, Evie will be thrilled when she finds out." My daughter doesn't have a shy bone in her body but being around a group of new people is still hard for her. Once she gets a conversation started or plays with someone, she's good, but she struggles to get to that point.

Caleb's daughters are in the same grade as Ben, so we discuss what they'll be up to this year for a few minutes before the teachers say they're ready to begin. Evie's standing in the same corner of the room she went to when we first walked in, her head and Sophie's close together and I'm sure they're plotting something.

Isaac sees it too. "Those two are probably planning world domination. Should we be worried?"

One side of my mouth tips up in a grin. "Two girls plotting together? We should definitely be afraid."

Before he can say anything else, Meredith steps forward, introducing herself for any parents who haven't been here before and I look around the room, cursing under my breath when I still don't see Tabitha. She told Evie she'd be here, but she's probably too busy with her friends or working on something she could easily put off for an hour or two to see what her daughter's been working on for the past few months.

Luckily it doesn't seem like Evie has even noticed. She's too busy following the stretching routine Meredith and her partner are doing. She's been in dance since she was four and it shows. She's so graceful. Her confidence in her dancing is clear for anyone to see and my heart swells with pride. That's my girl.

The dancers all run through their planned routines, starting with the youngest group. It's smart to get them out of the way before they get restless. Every time I come watch what Evie's teachers are doing, I'm blown away by how organized everything is.

Finally, Evie's group comes into the middle of the room and get into their formation. It almost looks like a diamond, and my daughter's in the middle with a big grin on her face.

They start to dance and I recognize the song as one from an animated movie that's practically been on repeat at my place since it came out. Evie loves it, and even Ben has sat down to watch it with her one of the four hundred times it's been on my television. Now I know why she's danced around the apartment humming to herself for weeks. The song sounded familiar, but she refused to tell me.

For a group of eight and nine-year-old girls, they do an amazing job moving in sync while Meredith counts out the beats to the music. My ex-wife does a lot that pisses me off, but picking this studio for our daughter was probably the best thing she ever could've done for her. Evie loves it here, and she loves Meredith and Jax.

Once her dance is done, Evie runs over with Sophie to stand and watch the older girls dance. I don't know Josie and Maddie well, but Evie idolizes them. She tells me again when she watches them dance, "Daddy, I want to be as good as Maddie when I grow up."

Caleb chuckles at her words. "You don't have too long before you're her age. Just keep practicing and I bet you'll be even better than you already are." Evie beams up at him.

"What about me, Uncle Caleb?" Sophie asks, staring up at him with a big smile on her face.

Leaning down, he tweaks her nose. "Of course you'll be amazing, Soph. How could you be anything but?" She giggles before turning her attention back to the dancers finishing up their routine.

The last group of dancers finally finishes their routine and Meredith walks into the middle of the room as the last person runs off to talk to all the parents and dancers.

"Hi, parents!" Her bubbly personality has everyone saying hi and smiling back at her. "I hope you all enjoyed that taste of our upcoming recital. All the kids have been working hard and we are so excited for you to see the final, polished product." She goes on to talk about the costumes and what each dancer needs in the different age groups while Evie listens like there's going to be a test at the end she's going to have to take.

My head is spinning by the time she stops speaking. Every year the recitals are more involved and there's more stuff for the parents to do. It's rough for parents like me who don't have anyone to help do things. Tabitha sure can't be counted on to help sew on sequins or hot glue feathers to fabric. At least it's been two years since the feathers thing. I think I still have PTSD from that. Feathers all over the damn house. I swear to God I found feathers for over a year after in the most random places.

"I'm gonna tell Miss Meredith bye," Evie tells me, not giving me the chance to tell her we need to get going. I'm sure Ben's had enough being at my parents. They're great, don't get me wrong, but she always finds him something to do while he's there so going to grandma's isn't the break for him it is for Evie.

Since she runs off, I have a few extra minutes to discuss the upcoming football season with the guys. Isaac and Caleb's brother is a player on our local team, so they have lots of inside info on who's still struggling with an injury or who's not going to do well this year. It will come in handy when we start picking fantasy players at the garage.

Evie finally runs back over to me ready to leave, and we're almost at the door when Meredith says my name. The look on her face instantly has my body on alert. She's about to say something I'm *not* going to like… I can tell.

"Mitch, if you need help with the costumes," she starts to say, but I cut her off.

The fact that she thinks I need help coming up with a

dance costume for my own kid ticks me off. "I've got it handled."

She can tell I'm not going to relent, so Meredith finally nods. "Okay. Let me know if anything changes. We'll be glad to help with anything you need." With one last smile at Evie, she walks off to speak to other parents and I take advantage of her leaving to do the same. I don't need or want any more offers of "help," especially if they come from some of the single moms in the group. Dating the parent of one of Evie's dance mates wouldn't end well for any of us.

CHAPTER 14

Hailey

oday is the day. My first day as a real, live teacher! I was so excited last night it was almost like *I* was about to be a student this year too.

My mom was entirely too happy to come and get Connor this morning though. There's no way I can thank her enough for being willing to drop everything to help me out, even if it kills me I'm not going to see him on his first day of pre-school.

Walking into my classroom, all I can do is turn circles in a crazy attempt to see everything one last time before my students come in. They're all going to love being in my classroom this year. It's so bright and cheerful, the two things I lived way too much of my life without.

Kids start filing into the room a few minutes later and I freeze. Literally, all I can do is stand here and stare at them all as they make their way to the desks with their names on them.

Can I really do this? I'm not sure. I was confident about this before I saw all the kids, but now that it's real, I'm actually going to be *teaching* kids, I'm panicking. Who gave me permission to shape young kids' minds? They were wrong.

Mitchell's daughter is one of the last girls to walk into the room and she runs right over to throw her arms around my waist. I instinctively hug her back, enjoying the feel of her warm body against mine as I take a couple of calming breaths.

"Hey, Ms. Lucas," she shrieks, voice shrill enough to shatter glass. "Look! This is my new outfit," she pulls the hem of her dress to show me, "and I got a new backpack too." Turning, she shows me the colorful bag on her shoulders.

I run my hand down her hair, smoothing the wild brown strands. "Very pretty. I love your dress." My agreement makes her smile get impossibly wide. Before I can tell her to take her seat, she turns her head and sees Sophie sitting at her own desk and shrieks her name too. She runs over to her and they start comparing each other's bags but take their seats when the bell sounds.

My first day goes by entirely too fast, and before I realize it, it's already time for the kids to pack up to go home. They've got so many papers to take with them and I don't envy the parents a bit for the cramps they're going to have in their hands later.

After dropping off the bus riders, I lead the rest of the

class to the front of the school where the car pick up line starts and wait with them to meet up with their parents.

I walk each student over to their cars and greet the parents quickly before they drive away. When it's Sophie's turn, Stacey is the one in the driver's seat and she's grinning when I open the door.

"Hey Sophie," she greets her daughter as she gets into the car. "How was your day?" Sophie immediately starts telling her about her friends and all the books she's found on the shelves in my room. I had to pry her away from them when it was time to go home. If she was allowed, I think Sophie might sleep here just to be close to them.

Once Sophie's settled into the back seat, her attention turns briefly to me. "Hey Hailey, how was she today?"

"She was great," I assure her. "I'm going to love having Sophie in my class this year. She's going to be a great help when it comes to picking out books for our class to read."

Stacey beams at her daughter before turning her attention back to me. "That's great. I know she's excited to be in your class, especially since she has Evie to play with too."

Evie's standing beside me making faces through the glass at Sophie and giggling when she returns them. Stacey's face is soft as she watches her daughter and it warms my heart to see a parent look at their child that way. So many kids don't have that, and I'm so glad Sophie does.

After waving goodbye, we go through the next few cars, and then a familiar truck pulls up. Evie gets so excited when she sees her dad, she starts to vibrate. Me on the other hand, I'm shaking, but not from excitement. I have to shove my hands in the pockets of my dress—and who doesn't love a dress with pockets? —to keep my anxiety from being noticeable.

Ignoring him is difficult, especially when he reaches across to open the door for Evie to climb in. I watch as she pauses on the console to give her dad a hug and a kiss before continuing into the back seat. As soon as his attention isn't focused on her, it turns right to me.

"Well hello, Ms. Lucas." His eyes look my body up and down, and I can feel the blush popping up on my skin. Bright red with a pale yellow dress isn't a good look for anyone, trust me.

I'm not sure why him saying my name with such formality affects me this way, but *god*, it's way more attractive than it should be. I have to clear my throat in order to greet him back. "Hi." I consider saying "Mr. Anderson," but that just makes me feel silly, so I don't.

"I like your dress." The grin on his face makes me blush harder, but I manage to thank him in spite of it. Words are hard when you're as embarrassed and out of sorts as I am right now. "How was the first day?"

Finally, his focus is more on his daughter than on me. "You should ask Evie, not me." I give him a little smile to take the sting out of my words, but he's completely oblivious.

"Oh, believe me, I'll be hearing about her day all evening." I was wrong to think he was concentrating more on his daughter, and that should irritate me to no end, but I'm enjoying the attention way too much. "Right now, I want to hear about *yours*."

We stare at each other, him waiting to hear and me

struggling not to engage with him until a horn honks a couple of cars back from his. A stormy look fills his face, but before he can unleash the temper I can tell he has, I take a step away, putting more distance between me and his truck. "Now's not a good time."

The look he gives me says this isn't over, but he doesn't have much of a choice. I can't stand here in the car line and carry on a conversation with him, no matter how much I want to. Deliberately, I turn my attention to Evie who's watching us in the back seat and give her a small wave and a smile. "See you tomorrow, Evie."

Even though I know I shouldn't, I look back at Mitchell and the smoldering look he's giving me makes me shiver. "Enjoy the rest of your day, Mr. Anderson." His eyes fill with an emotion I can't decipher, but he nods slightly, accepting the loss of whatever game he's trying to play with me.

"See you later, Hailey."

Gah... I love the way he says my name.

After all the car riders from my class are gone, I head back into the building so I can get my stuff together and get home to see Connor. That's the only thing I don't like about going to work. I'm so used to being with Connor every day and loved being a stay-at-home mom when Seth and I were still married, but I also know I'm going to love teaching. Just today has shown me that. Plus, he's loving what he calls "school" too, so I'm just going to count it all as a blessing. Things could be so much worse.

Picking Connor up doesn't take long. He's more than ready to go home after playing at daycare all day. The only fight we have when we walk into the apartment is what he's going to eat for dinner. The only thing he ever wants is chicken nuggets and fries, while I'd like to eat something a little healthier. Unfortunately, we compromise—he has chicken nuggets…I put together a salad from the limited offerings in the fridge.

Once he's bathed and in bed, I settle down on the couch with a very large glass of wine and the series I'm currently binge-watching. There's a lot of angst, and some very sexy vampires and I'm really enjoying it. In fact, I'm so engrossed in what's happening on the screen I let out a short scream when there's a knock at my door.

Who on earth would be showing up here at almost ten at night? Walking warily over to the door, I sneak a look through the peephole and almost scream again.

Mitchell? What is *he* doing here? I step away from the door, debating on whether or not I should answer it, and he knocks a second time. If I don't answer, he might start knocking louder and that could wake up my son.

I hurry to open the door and gasp when I see him. The peephole did *not* do him justice. He's wearing a pair of gray sweatpants—help me Jesus—and a black *Anderson Automotive* t-shirt that is stretched taut across his broad shoulders and muscled chest. Even the sleeves are struggling to contain his biceps.

Crossing his arms over said chest, he looks down at me and I start to fidget when his eyes darken. I look down at myself too and wince when I remember what I'm wearing. My dress was cute, but Connor tends to be a messy eater and both of us end up wearing about as much as he gets in his mouth sometimes. I changed into a tank top and shorts when we got home, and that tank top is still damp from his bath. White tank top plus water equals almost see-through, even if there's a built-in bra inside it.

My hair is also up in a messy bun now with pieces hanging down in my face and on my neck thanks to the wrangling I had to do to get him in and out of the tub. He loves it when he's in there, but Connor definitely does not like to give up playing time to get clean.

"Hey," I finally manage to say, crossing my arms over my chest in a futile attempt to keep him from seeing my nipples which are standing at attention now that he's in front of me.

The word barely leaves my lips when he lunges forward to grab me, pushing me into my apartment and somehow managing to close the door behind us before his mouth slams down on mine.

All I can do is hold on. Mitchell completely takes over when his mouth touches mine. His arms wrap around my waist, pulling me into the hard warmth of his body as his tongue demands entrance to my mouth. I'm helpless to resist him, and the first touch of his tongue to mine has a moan escaping my lips. He swallows it with his kiss and my knees buckle as his tongue strokes mine.

Kissing a man with a beard is a new experience for me. Seth was always clean-shaven, even a little anal about it. He didn't like scruff and would shave first thing in the morning and again right before bed. It was a little nuts.

Mitchell and his beard though? It's a strange experience. The hair is scratchy, but soft at the same time. It rubs against the sensitive skin on my face and adds another dimension to the kiss.

Our mouths move together like we've been kissing

forever. There's no clashing of teeth or both tilting our heads in the same direction. It's kind of magical the way we come together.

My arms reach up to wrap around his shoulders, and that's what breaks his concentration on our kiss. Before I know what's happening, he's released me and is now standing a foot or more away from me.

What just happened?

"*Fuck.*" Mitchell is staring at me like he's never seen me before and though my heart was just pounding because of our kiss, now it's pounding due to the regret I can see in his eyes and I brace myself for what I'm sure is about to be his rejection. "I didn't come here for that."

His words cause pain to splinter through my chest and I flinch. Mitchell takes a step forward but freezes when I take a step back. Meeting his eyes is hard, but I force myself to do it anyway. I'm not about to cower away from him when he's about to break my already shattered heart.

How does he have that kind of power over me already?

It shouldn't be possible. We barely know each other, but knowing he regrets what might be the best kiss I've ever had *hurts* something deep inside me and I snap.

"Don't." His mouth opens like he wants to say something, but I don't let him. "Just leave."

Instead of doing what I ask, he comes for me anyway, and even though I want to run from him, my body refuses to move this time. His hands come up to cup my jaw and he forces my eyes to stay on his. "*No.* I'm not going to walk away or let you walk away this time. You think I regret what happened, that kissing you wasn't the highest point in my year thus far. That couldn't be further from the truth."

I feel like I should protest, but his words are so sincere I can't even form the words to do it. *The highest point in his year.* Did he really just say that? Those words make me free like I'm floating, but I quickly come down to reality.

"What did you mean then? How many other ways can you mean it when you say you didn't come here for that?"

His eyes narrow in either frustration or aggravation… maybe a combination of the two. "It *means* I didn't come here to attack you, to force a kiss on you."

"You didn't do any of those things." His words have me so confused. Clearly, he didn't see that kiss the same way I did, something that's proven when he makes a disbelieving sound in reaction to what I say. Wanting to make him understand, I'm the one cupping his cheeks with my hands and forcing his attention to stay on me. "Mitchell, you *did not* attack me. Honestly, that was the best kiss I think I've ever had. I loved that you wanted to kiss me so much you couldn't control yourself."

This time he smiles. Maybe what I'm saying is getting through to him. "Best kiss you ever had, huh?" *Ugh.* Smug is way too good a look on him. I narrow my eyes to glare at him, refusing to say the words a second time. Once was plenty for his ego.

His arms slide down my back until they're resting at the top of my butt and we stand in the middle of my living room holding each other until reality intrudes in the form of Connor crying.

CHAPTER 15

Mitchell

*H*er son's crying breaks us apart and Hailey looks up at me, conflicted. "I need… I need to go see what's wrong with Connor. I'm sorry." Her shoulders slump, and I know she's telling me I need to go, but I'm not ready to do that yet, so I just nod, watching as she hurries down the short hallway away from me.

While she's murmuring to Connor and calming his cries, I walk around her small apartment, studying the pictures on the wall and the little accents that tell a lot about who she is.

The wall is covered with pictures of Connor, from a picture of her holding him just after his birth while looking both exhausted and radiant, to a picture of her with what must be her parents and by the similar coloring, her brother. She's smiling brightly in all the pictures she's in, but there is a definite dimming to it in the photos that are obviously the newest ones.

It makes me wonder exactly what her ex has done to her, and what he's still doing to her. Based on what she told me before, he must've cheated on her, and that makes me feel like an ass because I know she thinks I was going to use her to cheat on my now ex-wife. I have to figure out how to make her understand that until I met her, I had no interest in any type of relationship with another person. Helping me cheat on my wife isn't something I would ever ask of her... or anyone else for that matter.

Listening to her singing quietly to Connor has me feeling like I'm intruding, but I can't leave until I make her understand. I'm not sure how I'll do that, but if there's ever going to be any hope of us moving on together, I have to.

It doesn't take very long for Connor to settle, and Hailey is soon coming back down the hallway towards me, freezing when she sees me standing in front of the many photos on her wall.

"I thought you left," she says quietly, clasping her hands in front of her body like she's not totally sure what to do with herself.

As much as I want to go to her, I stay where I'm standing and give her the chance to come to me. If I go to her, this relationship—or whatever it is—is going to move to her bedroom long before she's ready. And that thought has me needing to adjust my pants. Wearing gray sweats around a girl who turns you on as much as Hailey does me is never a good idea.

When I don't immediately explain myself, Hailey tilts

her head to one side and studies me for a minute before going into her kitchen. I'm helpless to do anything but follow because I don't know what's going through her head.

Stretching high enough to lift the hem of her tank top to show a small strip of skin, she reaches into one of the upper cabinets and pulls down two wine glasses. After setting them on the counter, she goes to the fridge and grabs a bottle of wine and lifts it for my approval.

At my nod, she pours us both a glass and I grab them before she can, then follow her into the living room and take a seat on the couch beside her. She takes one glass from me and gulps some of the liquid down like she's hoping it will give her courage.

"So," she finally starts, looking down at the glass in her hands and avoiding me as much as she can, "if you didn't come here to kiss me, why did you come?"

I want her to look at me, but I don't want to force the issue. The whole reason she's avoiding my eyes is to protect herself and I get it. Now that I've got the chance to explain myself, to tell her exactly how I feel, the words are escaping me.

Hailey's waiting for me to speak, to tell her what's going on in my head, but I don't know how to start. Needing to say something, I blurt out the first thing that comes into my head. "You make it impossible for me to think rationally." As soon as I say it, I regret it because Hailey closes in on herself. "*Shit*. That's not what I meant."

"What did you mean then?" she asks, her voice barely a whisper of sound.

I fun a hand through my messy hair and try to think of

how to explain it to her. "When I'm around you, my brain just stops working. All I can think about is touching you, the way your hair smells, the way you feel against me."

Her face softens, and I breathe a sigh of relief. Now I'm finally getting somewhere. "I came over here tonight to find out about your day. Hailey, I find myself wanting to know everything about you. I want to know what you're thinking and why, how you feel about things, what your opinions are. Being around you is intoxicating."

The smile she gives me lights up the entire room along with every corner of my soul. "Oh Mitchell," she sighs. "That's the sweetest thing anyone has said to me in a long time." Her smile falls as she thinks of something and she doesn't make me wait to find out what it is. "But I'm your daughter's teacher. We can't have this type of relationship. It's not right, or fair to the other kids in my class."

"I don't think the kids in your class will care who you're dating, Hailey." She's crazy if she thinks I'm going to give her up now that I've found her again. That's not going to happen, no matter how much her being my daughter's teacher upsets people. I don't think it will though, as long as we aren't flaunting the relationship during school hours, which wouldn't happen anyway.

She huffs out an aggravated breath and I grin, loving that I'm getting to her. "It's not the kids I'm worried about, Mitchell, and you know it. It's the parents." Biting down on her lip, she thinks about what she wants to say next and I wait impatiently, wanting to hear what excuses she has for why we can't be together so I can dispute them. "This is my first year teaching. I can't risk my career just because you've decided we should be together."

Okay. Now I'm offended. "I'm not asking you to risk your career, Hailey." My words are clipped, and I sound more pissed off than I am. "The only thing I'm asking you for is a *chance*. I want the chance to show you how good I think we can be together. I haven't been able to stop thinking about you for a year, and I spent most of that year trying to find you. None of the people at Patsy's would give me any info on you, and the information on the form you gave when you dropped your car off that day must've been your old address because I couldn't find you that way either."

Hailey's mouth has dropped open and she's staring at me like she can't believe I'm real. "You looked for me?" I nod, unable to say the words a second time. I already sound like a fucking stalker. Her expression changes, eyes widening and a wide smile spreading her lips.

She looks like I just handed her the world and all I did was say a few embarrassing as hell words. Her body turns so she's almost facing me and I watch as she sets her glass down on the coffee table before bringing her hand up to cover her mouth. The trembling is obvious and I almost reach out to grab it, but manage to keep myself still. If I'd known telling her I went looking for her would have this kind of reaction, I would have opened with that the last time we were sitting on her couch like this.

"What did you expect, Hailey?" I finally ask her. "Did you think I would just forget you that day? That it wouldn't matter to me? I already told you it did, that *you* mattered."

She looks away from me and shrugs. "I don't know, I

just didn't expect you to put forth that kind of effort. Not for *me*."

The way she sees herself pisses me off, especially when I *know* her ex is the one who made her see herself that way. I just don't know *how*, and that's a conversation we need to have.

"This is probably the last conversation you want or expected to have tonight, but I think it's time you tell me about your ex. You know all about Tabitha, it's only fair I know about him." I should probably feel bad for putting her on the spot this way, but until she tells me, I won't know what damage he did to her while they were together. Based on the fact that she doesn't think she's worth any effort, he did a fucking lot. That asshole deserves every kind of pain I can dream up.

Hailey looks everywhere but at me. "I don't think we need to talk about him. He doesn't even factor into this discussion."

"I beg to differ." She's not getting off that easy. If I didn't think he mattered, I wouldn't have brought him up. "Like I said, you know about Tabitha and all the shit she pulled with me. I need to know about your ex too. We won't have the chance to build any kind of relationship if we don't put it all out there from the beginning."

Her head is shaking back and forth, making me think she's not about to tell me what I'm asking, but then she lets out a loud sigh that sends her bangs straight out above her eyes. "Fine. What do you want to know?" Her voice is petulant, and it makes me smile.

"Whatever you want to tell me." She scoffs, unable to believe I don't have some type of question. "Okay, fine.

What happened with him? Why did you split? You said a little bit, but you haven't really told me."

Now she shrugs, but a sad frown pulls at one side of her delectable mouth. "Same thing that happens in a lot of relationships probably. He was all happy when he found out I was pregnant with Connor, but it wasn't because he was excited to have a baby."

"What was he excited about then?" Her words are confusing.

Hailey pushes the hair falling in her face behind her ear self-consciously. "He was just happy he'd have an excuse to leave me at home when he went out with his friends. None of his friends had kids, so it was always him saying I should just stay home with the baby so I wouldn't be bored. If it wasn't that, it was that his friends' houses weren't baby-proofed or they were having an adult's only party. He always had an excuse for why I couldn't come with him." She looks right into my eyes when she continues, her chin coming up defiantly. "I finally decided that if I was going to have to do it all myself, I'd do it *by* myself too."

"I get that."

Her frown turns into a small smile and she looks down again. "The final straw was him refusing to come home when Connor was sick. He was running a high fever and coughing so much he was having trouble breathing. I was so scared, and he was too busy golfing with his buddies to come be with me. Thankfully, my mom came and sat with me at the hospital so I wasn't alone. I packed my stuff that weekend and was just about to leave when he got home." The tiny smile turns into a full-fledged grin. "He really wasn't happy about that. It was one thing for him to ignore me, but having to explain to his friends and business associates that I *left* him? That was unacceptable."

My hands turn into fists. "Did he hurt you?" I can barely get the words out around the anger crawling up my throat. Visions of beating the unknown dickhead fill my head and they don't stop until her soft hand covers my fist.

"No, not like that."

Hailey's shaking her head when I look at her, eyes wide as they watch me. I force myself to take deep breaths and try to calm down because I was a second away from going looking for him. "Good."

The way she's looking up at me like I'm some kind of hero for being worried about her ex hurting her has me going between two emotions. First, I want to beat the shit out of any man who treated her as anything other than the sweet, beautiful woman she is, and second, I want to pull her on top of me and show her with my body just how beautiful she is to me.

Knowing we aren't in that place yet, I gently remove her hand from mine and stand, rubbing my stiff palms on my sweatpants and hoping she doesn't notice the erection I'm trying unsuccessfully to keep hidden.

"I should probably go. The kids are home alone, and even though Ben is thirteen, he's still not mature enough to watch Evie for any length of time."

Hailey looks down at her watch and gasps. "Oh my gosh! I didn't realize you've been here so long. How long a drive do you have?"

She hasn't realized yet? "Uh, Hails? I live two buildings over."

Her shocked expression drains the tension out of me, and I lean forward to drop a kiss on her lips. As much as I want to deepen it, I manage to contain myself, and once we're standing at her door, I ask the question I originally came to ask. "Go to dinner with me Friday?

"What?" Her brows are furrowed when she looks up at me with a frown on her face. I can tell she's confused by the abrupt switch in the conversation.

"Will you go to dinner with me Friday?"

Her teeth bite down on her bottom lip and I almost groan at the sight. "Just dinner?"

"Sure, if that will get you to say yes." I have zero shame.

Hailey lifts one delicate brow and one side of her mouth tips up in a grin. "Okay. Dinner."

Her agreement makes me feel about ten feet tall. "Awesome." Holding up my phone, I ask, "What's your number?" She rattles it off and I call her to make sure it saves… and a little to see if her phone rings inside the apartment which it does. That way I know she's not planning to blow me off.

"See you later, sweetheart." Without giving her the chance to respond, I leave her apartment, shutting her door behind me. Friday can't come soon enough.

CHAPTER 16

Hailey

*I*t's been two days since I agreed to go on a date with Mitchell and I'm still trying to figure out what made me say yes. Now here we are with tomorrow being Friday and I *still* haven't asked my parents about watching Connor. I'm a little afraid to ask because I know my mom will grill me on why and what I'm going to be doing.

As much as I don't want to, now that I've picked up Connor from daycare I'm going over there to get it over with. He's been sitting in the backseat talking to himself since we left, and I have no idea what he's saying.

We pull into my parent's driveway and as soon as he realizes where we are he starts yelling for Granny and Pops like they're going to hear him from inside the house and come running for him.

Honestly, he's probably not far off. I swear my mom sits at the window and stares each day hoping we'll stop by because I haven't even turned the car off and she's on her way out to meet us.

"Hey sweetie," she says as she opens Connor's door to get him out. I'm not dumb enough to think she's calling me sweetie. I practically ceased to exist when I pushed him out. I'm pretty sure if it came down to me or Connor, she'd save him and not be a bit sorry.

The woman doesn't even wait for me to get out of the car before she's taking my son down the driveway to her house, talking to him the entire way. All I can do is watch them and shake my head. At least I know where I stand.

When I walk into the house I can hear her still talking to him and have to follow her voice to find them. They're in the living room, and she's dragging out all the toys she keeps here at her house like he's not capable of dumping the bin himself. I roll my eyes and walk over to where they are, coming to a stop beside my mom.

"Hey, mom."

She finally stands, brushing invisible lint off her pants as she does before finally turning to greet me with a hug. "Hi, honey. How was your day?"

Now that Connor's fully engrossed in playing with his blocks, she walks across the room and into the kitchen, leaving me to follow behind her.

"Are you guys staying for dinner?" She's distracted, pulling out the ingredients for whatever she's planning to make.

I lean over her shoulder to see what she's got. "Depends. Whatcha making?"

"I'm thinking chicken and rice. Your dad will hate that it isn't steak and so will your brother, but they both need to watch how much red meat they eat." She's got a point. I'm pretty sure my brother would live off only steak and mashed potatoes, if he could.

Knowing my brother is coming over means I need to get the asking over with. If he hears, he'll be worse than my mom. I wouldn't put it past him to show up at my apartment on Friday night just to grill Mitchell on his intentions. I swear Henry thinks I'm still fifteen. He's way too overprotective.

"Um, hey…Mom?"

She's distracted, still taking stuff out to make dinner. "Mmhmm?" Maybe asking while she's busy is better. At least, that's what I'm hoping.

"Can you watch Connor Friday night?"

I hold my breath, hoping she doesn't ask why, but I'm not that lucky. She stops rooting around in the fridge to look over at me. "Why? What's Friday?" Her eyes go up and to the left like she's thinking about things she might have missed, but she frowns when she comes up with nothing.

"It's not a big deal." *Please drop the interrogation.* I wave her off with a hand but it doesn't deter her. She just turns fully to face me and waits for me to spill. My shoulders sag in defeat and I sigh. "Okay, fine. I have a date."

Mom's entire face lights up and she smiles. "A *date*? With *who*? Do I know him?" She doesn't even give me a chance to answer her questions before she asks more. "What are you doing? Where are you going? What kind of date?"

"Mom!" I have to speak loudly to be heard over her and she snaps her mouth shut with a sheepish shrug of one shoulder. We both know she's not ashamed. The woman has *no* shame when it comes to her kids... or anything else for that matter. "Like I said, it's a date. We're going to dinner. No, you don't know him."

The way she's staring at me lets me know she doesn't by my nonchalance for a second. "Name?"

Grrr. "Mitchell."

"Mitchell what?"

Her eyes never leave me, and I start to squirm under her scrutiny. The way she's staring at me makes me feel like a teenager about to go on her first date. It's a strange feeling when you're a twenty-nine-year-old divorced mom yourself. "Mitchell Anderson," I finally relent and tell her.

The way her eyes light up and I want to kick myself. She knows who he is. *Crap.*

"Oooh, he's cute!"

My eyes roll at her description. *Cute* is not the word I'd use to describe him. Hot, sexy, sex on legs... any of those work better than *cute*.

"He's not a puppy, Mom. How do you know him?"

This time, she's the one waving me off. "Your dad has been taking his cars to Mitchell Automotive for as long as I've known him. He's good friends with Mitchell's dad. They always hoped the two boys would be friends even though Mitchell's a few years older than your brother. They never really got on though."

She shrugs like this isn't a big deal, but I can't help but wonder why my brother, who gets along with *everyone*, doesn't get along with Mitchell. Did I make a mistake saying yes to him? Kissing him?

Oh God, what have I done?

My mom doesn't notice my panic. She's still too busy swooning at the thought of me going on a date with him. "Of course, we'll watch Connor honey. Have fun... and don't do anything I wouldn't do." She winks as she says this last part and I want to hurl. I will never be old enough to think about my mom and sex in the same sentence.

The front door shuts, and my brother's voice yelling for our mom ends our conversation. I don't know if I should be happy or not, because the likelihood of her telling Henry about my date is much higher since she knows the guy.

My older brother walks into the kitchen and stops to kiss both me and mom on the cheek before grabbing a handful of cookies out of the jar on the counter. This action earns him a glare from her because, "Can't you see I'm in the middle of making dinner?"

He shrugs, completely unrepentant. "I already ate, so I'm allowed to have cookies."

"Where's Marisa?" I look back towards the living room, but I don't see or hear her or their two kids.

Henry doesn't even pause in his chewing to swallow before answering me. "They're at home. I came to see if Mom was up for babysitting this weekend so I can take my wife out for dinner."

Oh no... I hope he isn't planning for Friday.

"What day?"

My luck sucks because he does, in fact, say, "Friday." I

squeeze my eyes shut and *pray* mom doesn't tell him, but as I said, my luck *sucks*.

After debating for a second, mom finally tells him, "Friday should be fine. I'm already watching Connor for your sister. Bring the twins over and they can all play together." She completely disregards the fact that two seven-year-old girls probably won't want to play with their three-year-old male cousin. They're not exactly into the same toys.

His attention turns to me. "Why's she watching Connor?"

"Your sister has a *date*," Mom tells him this in a sing-song voice, beaming her happiness at me and I inwardly cringe because I know what's about to come.

"A date? With who?" Henry sounds pissed at just the prospect, so I'm dreading him finding out who it is.

I wouldn't put it past him to show up at my apartment before I leave to put the fear of God into Mitchell. Sometimes having a big brother sucks. Where was he when Seth was trying to date me? He could've saved me some heartache. Well, that's not totally true. I wouldn't trade having Connor for anything, but I would definitely change who his father is if I had the chance.

"Mitchell Anderson," I mumble, hoping he lets it go, but of course he doesn't.

Eyes narrowing as he looks at me, Henry grits out, "I know you didn't just say Mitchell Anderson."

"Henry!" Mom chastises him. "Mitchell is a perfectly nice man, and handsome too."

He snorts in disbelief. "Yeah, nice and *married*."

I jump in to defend him. "He's not married anymore. Mitchell got divorced last year."

"Even if he did," Henry allows, "you deserve better."

His statement confuses me. I mean, I'm his sister, so of course, he wants the best for me. But, what does he know about Mitchell that makes him think he doesn't deserve me? I have so many questions right now. "Well, it doesn't matter anyway. It's only one date. For all we know, it won't even go anywhere."

I'm trying to play it off, but I don't think I'm successful based on the look Henry gives me. Thankfully, he lets the subject drop and is gone by the time we sit down to eat. It doesn't stop me from worrying about this date and if I'm being stupid by going out with him. All I can do is hope it doesn't cause me more heartache because I've had enough of that to last a lifetime.

CHAPTER 17

Mitchell

Friday is finally here and I feel like I've been waiting forever for it to get here instead of just a couple of days. I'm glad this week was one where Tabitha has the kids for the weekend so I didn't have to try to have my parents watch the kids. Ben would've given me all kinds of shit because he's convinced he's old enough to be the babysitter, but even at thirteen, I don't think he's mature enough.

After sitting in my silent, empty apartment for the last two hours like a loser, it's finally time to head over and get Hailey. I hope she likes where I chose for our date tonight. Choosing someplace to take her was hard. Trying to balance wanting to be able to talk to her and not wanting it to seem like I'm trying too hard to impress her.

It might make me a pussy to say this, but I want her to

like *me*, not what I can do for her or where I can take her. That was always the problem with Tabitha. She was way too focused on appearances and I always felt like I fell short with her.

Hailey doesn't make me wait when I knock on her door. She almost opens it before I've finished knocking and I can't help but grin down at her. With her blonde hair curling over her shoulders and wearing skinny jeans with a band t-shirt it's clear she took my "be comfortable" reply to her text asking where we were going tonight.

Returning my smile, she shuts the door behind her and there's so little room between us her back is right up against it. Her positioning makes kissing her easy so I take advantage. A gentleman would wait until the end of the date to try to steal a kiss, but I never professed to be one of those.

The kiss is way too short and I'm regretting not deepening it when I straighten. A pretty pink flush graces her cheeks and her eyes are still closed. As much as I'd love to keep this going, I promised her a date and I intend to deliver.

With that thought in mind, I take her hand in mine and lead her down to my truck. I may not be a gentleman, but I'll damn sure open doors for her and help her delectable ass up into my truck.

The ride to the restaurant is relatively quiet, and I start to second guess my choice the longer it takes to get there. Maybe I'm wrong and she is the type of girl to expect fancy, expensive dinners. I don't think she is though, and soon we're pulling into the parking lot so it's too late to second guess anything.

Hailey leans forward when she sees where we are, and when she looks back over at me her eyes are sparkling with joy. "Red Mill Burgers? I *love* this place. They don't serve chicken nuggets so Connor won't eat here, but their milkshakes are *so* good. I can't remember the last time I was here."

I let out a breath I didn't even know I was holding and we head into the thankfully not too busy restaurant. It's surprising for a Friday night, but they're also really good at getting people in, fed and out quickly.

We take our seats and give the waitress who comes over our drink orders before an awkward silence settles over us. It's the first time things between us haven't been easy and I have to say, I'm a little surprised. I'm struggling to find a way to start a conversation and end up saying the first thing that comes to mind.

"So, Nash?"

Hailey looks at me questioningly, then when she sees my focus, looks down at her shirt, and smiles. "Yeah, they're my favorite band. Leo Nash is so hot." She fans herself while she says this and the naughty grin on her face says she knows exactly what she's doing to me.

"Oh yeah? What's so hot about him?" My jealousy spikes and her telling me how hot some other guy is, even if he's a celebrity, makes me want to hulk out and show her I'm the only guy she should be thinking is sexy.

She sighs longingly and I want to take her over my knee for teasing me like this. "His piercings, his tattoos… those stars are just *yum*."

Well, I have tattoos too. I tell her this, but she just laughs. "I know, I can see them." The way she says it makes me envision her sticking her tongue out after and she does just that. She doesn't stick it out far, but enough I know she's doing it.

Crossing my arms over my chest, I glare at her until she snickers. "I'm much better looking than he is." Why I'm trying to compare us I will never know.

"Eh," she says, holding up a hand and moving it back and forth in a so-so motion.

After a couple of seconds, Hailey can't keep a straight face and starts giggling. "Sorry. You're just so easy to wind up, I couldn't help it."

"Uh-huh." I probably look like I'm pouting, but I'm not. It's cute that she's trying to get me all riled up, and I'll be sure to return the favor the first chance I get.

Before we can talk anymore, the server brings our food and Hailey's stomach growls loudly. She ducks her head in an attempt to hide her blush, but I can still see it. "Good thing we got here when we did."

"Shut up," she mutters with a laugh before shoving a fry into her mouth. Hailey lets out a small moan at the taste of her food and I have to start thinking of very non-sexy things so I don't sprout wood right here at the table. That would be hard to explain to our waitress.

We're halfway through our food when a shadow crosses our table, and when I look up, I see Isaac, along with his brothers Matt, Caleb and Will. "Hey man," he greets me before turning to Hailey. "And Ms. Lucas, what are you doing with this joker?"

She doesn't answer, and when I look over, she's staring at Will with her mouth and eyes wide open. Will's grinning down at her like she's the most amusing thing he's seen today and his brothers' are all rolling their eyes.

"Hey," Will says to her, holding out a hand for her to shake.

Hailey's still frozen, but just as him holding his hand out turns awkward, she shakes herself out of it and manages to put her hand in his with a soft, "H-h-hey." His grin widens when she continues to stutter. "You… you're Will Montgomery." Her voice is full of awe.

Isaac chuckles. "Don't remind me." Leaning closer to her, he tells Hailey, "He already has a big head, don't make it any worse."

"Fuck off," Will says, shoving him out of the way so he can focus back on her. "Are you a fan?"

She finally snaps out of whatever fantasy she's playing out in her head and grins. "I'm not, but my dad and brother are huge fans. They've been talking about getting season tickets for years but it never happens." Hailey snickers. "They're going to be *so* mad I met you tonight."

"Well then," Will looks over at me out of the corner of his eye and smirks. "Guess we need to take a picture so you'll have proof, huh?" Nodding, Hailey gets up and goes over to stand beside him. Will puts his arm around her and asks, "Where's your phone?"

Fumbling, she pulls it out of her pocket and shows it to him and he nods to me. "Take our picture, man?"

Hailey's giddy as she stands beside him and even though I want to punch him for touching her, I'm glad she's enjoying herself so I take the phone and stand myself.

It takes a few minutes to get a good shot because while

Hailey's tall, Will still towers over her and I swear he's milking it for all he's worth just to get a rise out of me.

Finally, he decides on a pose where he's got one arm around her and the other is flexing his bicep while he gives me a smile that shows all his teeth. Hailey's standing beside him with a big grin on her face too, but unlike him, she's not hamming it up for the camera. She looks slightly uncomfortable, like she's not sure where to put her arms or if she's allowed to touch him at all.

By the time we get a picture that Will agrees is "good enough" we've been standing here blocking the aisle for close to ten minutes and my patience for her being touched by someone who isn't me is at an end.

Grabbing her hand, I pull her away from Will so her back is against my chest, then drop her hand in favor of putting mine on her hip. Everyone in Seattle knows Will is happily married, but my sudden caveman brain isn't capable of understanding that.

I know Isaac understands when he nods and elbows Will in the side. "C'mon man, let's go so these two can finish their dinner."

"Oh, it's okay—" Hailey starts, but I interrupt.

"Good idea. Have a good night." She tips her head back to glare at me, but she's so adorable it's extremely ineffective and only makes the guys standing close to us chuckle.

They all give their goodbyes and we are left to sit and finish our food in peace.

CHAPTER 18

Hailey

The rest of dinner is pretty quiet. Mitchell talks about different cars he's been working on and I tell him some of the funny things students have done this week at school. I still can't get over how easy it is to talk to him and how much I like just listening to him too. It feels like I've known him forever, but when you add up how much time we've actually spent talking to each other, it's not very long at all.

After we've paid, we leave the restaurant and he helps me into his truck. While I wait for him to come around to the driver's side I can't help but wonder what we're going to do next. Is he going to take me home and say see ya bye? Is he expecting an invitation to my bed? *Oh God,* what if he is? I don't know how I'll answer if that's the case.

He's in the truck before I can obsess too much, and once he starts it, he turns to face me. "I don't know about you, but I'm not ready for tonight to end."

I practically sag in my seat in relief. "I'm not either."

"Good." He grins before pulling out of the parking lot. "I know just the place."

It doesn't take very long, and when we pull into the next parking lot I start to laugh. "Bowling? *Really*?"

Mitchell shrugs. "Why not? Bowling is fun." I give him a look that says I'm not sure it's fun and he just smirks. "I mean, if you're worried I'm going to beat you, we can always play pool instead."

"Ha! I'm not sure that's fair either. Pool isn't something I'm very good at." Truth is, I did a lot of bowling when I was younger and was decent. I'm not about to tell him that though. Let him think I'm worried about losing and maybe he'll take it easy on me.

The place is busy when we walk in, but there are a few open lanes. Not many, but a few. We get our shoes and pick out our balls, then I follow him over to the lane they gave us. After putting on the ugly bowling shoes, we program the screen that will show our scores and it's time to start.

I'm distracted at first because this bowling alley is new to me and has a serious hipster vibe. Mitchell looks very comfortable here with his beard and tattoos, not that I would ever call him a hipster to his face. And he's not one, he just comes off as being very laid-back and easygoing.

He does have his intense moments though. When we were still at the restaurant and I was taking the picture with Will, his eyes were almost *burning* with possessiveness. I'd be lying if I said it didn't make the spot between my thighs damp and needy. It was awesome considering I haven't been attracted to *anyone* in so long. Seth sure never made me feel that way. With him, I was always either an inconvenience or an afterthought.

Mitchell lines up his first shot and his ass in those jeans drags my attention away from the high ceilings and exposed beams. I stare shamelessly at the picture him bent over presents, struggling not to reach up and check for drool in the corner of my mouth. He's got *such* a nice butt. It's the kind you just want to take a bite out of.

Said butt turns and I try to focus my attention on *anything* else, but he catches me staring. "Like what you see?"

My face bursts into flames, but I force myself to meet his gaze and say something I normally wouldn't. "Uh, *yeah*. Anyone who says they don't is lying."

His head drops back as he bursts into laughter and I watch his Adam's apple bob beneath his beard. *Gah*. It should be illegal to be as attractive as he is. It's not fair. How is a girl supposed to keep from tumbling straight from lust into love when he's standing there looking like a god with his tall, broad-shouldered, lean-waisted body?

It's a struggle, but I manage to turn my attention away from his body to look up at the score. He got a strike while I was ogling him like a crazy obsessed stalker. *How* did he concentrate long enough to do that?

Mitchell's still grinning at me when I turn back to him and I know he knows what I'm thinking. He doesn't acknowledge it though, he just gestures for me to take my turn and I do my best to put on a show. I want him to be just as distracted as I am.

I make a show of swinging my hips when I walk up to grab my ball and bend over slowly, hopefully giving him the *best* view of my butt in these jeans. This wasn't what I imagined our date was going to be like when I got dressed, but the skinny jeans and t-shirt I decided on are working out very well. It also doesn't hurt that my… let's say *admiration* of Leo Nash made Mitchell get a very jealous and possessive glint in his eyes.

Mitchell's groan when I bend to release the ball has me hiding a smile when I turn back to face him. It's killing me not to watch the ball as it rolls down the alley, but I'm trying to act confident and sexy instead of insecure and whatever the opposite of sexy is. Frumpy? Maybe, but I wouldn't say I feel frumpy. That could just be the way he's so laser-focused on the sway of my hips as I walk back to where he's sitting.

The sound of pins falling stops me right before I reach him, and all thoughts of pretending to be cool desert me as I spin around and stare up at the screen. It only takes a few seconds before my pin count loads on the screen, but I feel like I'm holding my breath when I watch. I could just look down to the end and count, but that takes all the anticipation out of it.

Squealing when the "X" for a strike fills the first box I bounce a little on my toes and clap for myself, grin widening further when I hear his tortured-sounding groan from behind me. I'm not sure if it's because we're tied or the movement I know my butt and boobs makes when I bounce.

Turning, I see Mitchell sitting in one of the uncomfortable plastic chairs, his eyes not leaving my face which feels very deliberate. I practically skip over to take my own seat so he can take his next turn and smirk over at him. "This is going to be interesting."

He looks at me, almost like he's shocked I'm taunting him, then laughs. "Yes, yes it will. We should make a bet."

"What kind of bet?" The possibilities have me intrigued and I wonder what he's planning.

His own smile lifts one side of his mouth as he thinks. "Winner's Choice? It can be a surprise."

"Deal," I hurry to agree, liking the fact that I'll have some time to figure out what I want from him *when* I win.

The rest of the game goes by way too fast, and by the time we get to the last frame I'm winning by nine and already planning what I want for my prize. In the last frame, Mitchell gets *three* strikes. I'm starting to think he's not been honest in his playing because before this frame he had three strikes and four spares. I've had three turns where I had gutter balls on either the first or second throw which have sort of canceled out my three spares in a row at the beginning of the game and the two I had in frames eight and nine.

Eight flashes on the screen when I throw the ball and I deflate a little bit. Eight isn't very competitive when compared with his strikes, but when the screen shows what pins are left I can see I still have a chance at getting a spare. The remaining two are grouped together which is way better than having them spread out.

My body tenses when I feel his chest brush against my

back just before his breath hits my ear. "You missed a couple."

"It's only the first one. There's still time for me to beat you." I'm pretty proud of myself because my voice sounds normal. Especially since it's taking everything I have not to melt into a puddle at his feet. His heat is surrounding me and I feel like I'm drowning in the intoxicating scent of his cologne mixed with the scents of motor oil and *man*. That's the only way I can think to describe it.

Moving forward, I take my second shot, and this time I stand at the edge of the lane to watch as it travels down. My body leans to the right like I can somehow move the ball psychically or something and Mitchell chuckles at my actions. I turn my head for a second to glare at him, and it sounds like he's strangling himself when he swallows back more laughter.

The ball hits the pins and they both fall, giving me a spare. I fist pump the air and rub my hands together in glee as I wait for my ball to come back and when it does, I walk carefully to the edge of the lane and take a deep breath.

C'mon Hailey, you can do this. Get a strike!

The ball leaves my hand and I stand at the edge once more and hold my breath. Watching the ball go down is nerve-wracking and I'm praying to every God I know to please, *please* let me get a strike.

I watch the ball get closer and closer until it finally crashes into the pins, knocking every single one of them down. As soon as I realize I got my strike, I spin around and run *carefully* back to watch the screen tally our final scores.

Mitchell comes to stand behind me right as the scores flash above us. *One hundred and seventy-eight.* I beat him by *one* point.

Before I analyze it too much, I turn, throw my arms around Mitchell's neck and press my lips to his. His arms wrap around my waist and he takes over, pressing his mouth against mine harder. He traces the seam of my mouth with his tongue until I sag against him and let him in. It feels like he's taking me over. This isn't just a kiss, it's a *conquering*.

The noise and the people around us fade away until it's just the two of us standing here in this embrace. I'm surrounded by him, his arms the only thing keeping me upright at this moment. Mitchell's tongue is stroking mine and when he pulls it back into his own mouth, mine follows eagerly. I swear, I could kiss this man forever and be happy.

Slowly, the sounds around us penetrate our little bubble and Mitchell straightens, breaking the connection of our mouths. He's looking down at me when I open my eyes and all I can see is the evidence in them of how much he wants me... or maybe I'm seeing that because I can feel the erection in his pants pressing against my stomach. Either way, knowing how much he wants me makes me bold and I reach up to kiss him again.

This time, I'm the one who pulls away when I hear someone clear their throat, embarrassment filling every inch of my body.

"Can I help you?" Mitchell asks, voice gravelly like he's got something in his throat.

The shorter man standing to our side looks just as

uncomfortable as I am, but he stands his ground. "I'm going to have to ask you to take all of that," he waves his hand at us like we won't understand what "that" is, "outside." Lifting his chin, he looks steadily at Mitchell. "This is a family-friendly establishment." Now he sounds scandalized and as hard as I try I can't keep the giggle from escaping.

Covering my mouth with both hands, I try to contain myself, but my giggles turn into almost hysterical laughter. How is this my life right now?

"No problem," Mitchell assures him. "We were just about to leave anyway."

The guy, who I'm guessing is the manager on duty since he sure didn't offer up any information on who he is, continues to stand in our area while we put our shoes back on and get ready to go. Mitchell grabs my shoes with his to take them back and the guy reaches out and takes them.

"I'll take care of these for you."

Dang. He must be anxious for us to leave his counter. The thought kills any mirth remaining in my body so I can only feel the mortification at being chastised like a child by this guy who isn't even as tall as I am.

As soon as I'm ready, Mitchell leads me out of the building and when we're both in the car he turns to look at me out of the corner of his eye. "You're trouble, you know that?"

I gasp. "*I'm* trouble? How do you figure that?"

"You're the one who kissed me," he says with a shrug. "What was I supposed to do?"

His head fully turns to face me and he winks, making

my giggles start up again. "I can't believe we essentially got kicked out of there for *kissing*. That guy acted like we were about to start sexing it up in the middle of the lane or something."

"Well," Mitchell muses, rubbing his chin with one hand like he's contemplating what I said. "I wouldn't have turned that down. Was that one of the options?"

Smacking his arm, I snicker harder. "*No way*. That kinda stuff is only done behind closed doors." Wait… he's not into public sex, is he? That is *so* not my thing.

"Don't worry, that won't ever happen. I'm not the type of guy who shares, not even to have someone watch us."

With that, he reaches over and takes my hand in his, the discussion over. His hand holding mine is so nice. I can feel the callouses on his fingers from all the manual labor he does, and it only makes him sexier to me. Seth's hands never felt that way. His were always soft, maybe even softer than mine, and I wouldn't put it past him to get manicures every week or two either.

It's later than I thought when we pull into the apartment parking lot and I'm right back in panic mode. Do I invite him in? Does he even *want* to come in? Is he *expecting* to come in? So. Many. Questions.

I'm not sure if I'm doing a good job hiding my anxiousness or if he just doesn't notice, but Mitchell doesn't make any comments when he helps me out of his truck by holding my trembling hand. Even our walk up to my door is silent. It makes me freak out more because I don't know what's going through his head or how to tell him what's going through mine.

Mitchell leans against my doorjamb while I search

through my bag for my keys and I take longer than I need to because I'm waiting for him to make a move one way or the other. I don't want to make a move, especially if it's the wrong one, and I'm just not confident enough to put myself out there by inviting him in or by telling him I'm not ready for that.

The decision is taken out of my hands once I pull out my keys and unlock my door. Mitchell opens it for me, then grabs my hand to pull me around to face him. He takes my face in his hands and leans down to press a soft, sweet kiss to my lips. It's so different from the others we've had tonight and if anything, it makes me want to sink further into his embrace.

He's the one who pulls back first and stares down at me, his eyes searching mine. I'm not sure what he sees, but he smiles gently before giving me one final kiss. "I really enjoyed tonight, Hailey."

"Me too, Mitchell."

After tucking a piece of hair behind my ear, he steps back. "As much as I want to come in with you, I also want to do this right so I'm going to say good night."

"You are?" My voice is breathy, and I hate that it sounds that way, but I'm too relieved to dwell on it. "I want to do this right too."

He's still smiling at me when he says, "Sweet dreams, Hails. I'll talk to you tomorrow."

"Sweet dreams, Mitchell."

He waits for me to go inside and shut the door behind me, and once I flip the locks, I watch him leave out the peephole before turning so my back is against the wood. I'm grinning like a loon, but I can't bring myself to care.

CHAPTER 19

Mitchell

I want nothing more than to go knock on her door this morning, but I know I need to give her a little space. By the time we got back here last night she was starting to freak out and I hate that she felt that way. I didn't know what to do to make it better, so I didn't say anything at all until we were at her apartment. I would've loved to end my night with her in bed beside me, but I don't want to push her too far too fast. I'm not completely convinced she's forgiven me for last year, and until I know for sure she has I'm not going to take that step with her.

Since I can't see who I really want, I head over to my parents. I haven't seen them in a few weeks and mom's been leaving messages on my voicemail asking me when I'm going to stop by every day for the last week and a half.

She probably has something she wants me to help dad do, which is a good thing this morning. Physical labor will keep my mind off Hailey.

Dad's out in the front yard when I get there and waves when he sees me. He's standing in front of one of the trees, his hand rubbing his beard at his chin over and over as he thinks. It's something he's done for as long as I can remember and the sight is a little bit comforting. It's nice to know some things never change.

"What are you doing?"

He shrugs. "Nothing, just looking."

"At?"

His eyes cut to me and I have to laugh at how peeved he looks. "At whatever keeps me out of the house and from doing all the shit on your mother's never-ending to-do list." Shaking his head, he mutters, "Why did I ever retire?"

It's so hard to keep from laughing. Mom's the one who wanted him to retire, and he finally completely retired six months ago so she'd stop complaining about how he'd rather be at the shop than with her. Dad's always been the type to stay busy, but I'm sure her list is full of busy work and he's not going to be interested in doing any of that.

"You retired because you wanted to spend more time with mom."

Dad snorts. "No, I retired because she wouldn't stop nagging me to spend time with her. There's a difference."

"Well, either way, you're home now. And, I'm sure whatever it is she wants you to do is stuff that does need to be done, so isn't it better to just get it over with?"

Narrowing his eyes, he glares at me. "Whose side are you on here?"

"Mom's, obviously. She's the one who sends me home with cookies and food so I don't have to make dinner."

He "hmphs" at me, but he knows it's true. That's the reason he's here too. Mom is a damn good cook and if he doesn't do what she wants, she's not going to let him have any of the goodies I'm sure she's in the house making.

Before he can say anything else, Mom comes to the door and looks out at both of us. "What are you guys doing out here? I have lunch ready, Mitch, if you're hungry."

"Of course, I'm hungry," I tell her as I'm walking up the front walk. "When am I not?"

She laughs, and when I reach the door, I wrap my arms around her and hug her. Mom hugs me back just as tightly, then moves so I can walk inside.

"What brings you over today?" She's looking up at me like she already knows why I'm here, but I don't know why she would.

I keep walking through the house because the smell of the food she made is making my stomach growl, but toss back over my shoulder, "Food. I'm here for the food."

Entering the kitchen, I can see she's been cooking like she's expecting an army, something that tells me for sure she knew I was going to come over today. It's not just sandwiches or something either. Nope, she made country fried steak, mashed potatoes, peas, and biscuits.

My mouth starts to water when I see all the food and I almost drop to my knees and thank God for moms who love to cook and do it every damn day.

She waits until I've filled a plate and taken my seat at the table before she sits down across from me and stares. *Damn it.* The look she's giving me is the same one she gave when I was seven and broke one of the lamps in the living room. She knew it was me the whole time, no matter how much I swore it wasn't. It's the same look she gives me when she knows she can break me easily because it's the stern type of look all mothers seem to know exactly when to use.

"What?" It comes out defensive and short and I regret it immediately when her look turns into a glare. My mom is the *best* at making a thirty-eight-year-old man feel like he's ten again.

My shoulders roll forward, so I'm hunched over my plate and looking anywhere but her when she speaks. "I hear you had a date last night."

"How did you hear that?" I ask, then grimace. That makes it sound like I was trying to keep it a secret, which isn't the case. She's been trying to get me to date people since pretty much the second Tabitha and I split up. I didn't want to tell her about Hailey because finding out I talked to someone before the split with her happened will only disappoint her.

The look she gives me, her chin dipping down as she looks at me from under her lashes, tells me she thinks I'm an idiot, which is confirmed when she says, "Becky Ellis called me last night and said you were out with her daughter. Imagine my surprise because you haven't said a word to anyone. Having someone else tell me what my son is up to was so embarrassing, Mitchell James."

I cringe at her saying both my first and middle names.

At least she didn't throw out all three names though. I'm not in *too* much trouble. How do I explain this to her without telling her everything? "I'm sorry, Mom. Maybe I should've told you, but it was just a first date." Inspiration comes and I tell her, "I didn't want to get your hopes up until I knew whether or not it was going to go further than one dinner."

"You better have done more than take her to dinner." She smacks my hand since it's the only part of my body she can reach. "Although," she muses, "I guess it's better than doing just a movie. At least you can talk during dinner." Looking off to some unknown point, she continues. "I'm trying to think, have I ever met Hailey? Since she grew up I mean. She was such a pretty little girl, and a pretty teenager too."

The woman is baiting me, and I know it, but I go along with it anyway. "She's still beautiful. I don't remember her from when I was younger, but she's definitely the prettiest woman I've ever seen."

The smile Mom gives me is wide, and so bright it could power the sun. "Good! So, tell me all about her." She's settling in for the long haul, but I'm hungry, my food is getting cold, and I don't want to dissect my date with my mother.

"Mom," I groan. "How bout this? If it goes further than just last night, I'll bring her over and you can see for yourself how great she is. Okay?"

She looks scandalized. "*If*? What do you mean if? You didn't ask her out again last night when you dropped her off? Did you at least talk to her this morning?"

Before I can answer, my dad's voice comes from the

kitchen and sounds like he has a mouth full of food. "Woman, leave the boy alone. He was married for Christ's sake. I think he knows how to woo a female without your assistance."

I try, I *really* do, but I can't keep from laughing at the scowl and glare she gives the empty doorway. When he doesn't come into the dining room, she gets up and goes to him and I listen to them bicker back and forth while I finish my lunch. Hearing them argue good-naturedly brings back so many memories of my childhood, and that's exactly what I need today.

CHAPTER 20

Hailey

*I*t's been a week since the best date I've ever had, but aside from some very hot looks he's given me during pick up this week and a couple of texts exchanged, I haven't spent any time with him. I shouldn't feel like I'm going through withdrawals, but *I do*. The whole thing is so crazy.

His wife "had" to bring the kids back on Sunday though instead of keeping them until their scheduled switch date, so that has a lot to do with it too. He can't just leave his son at home babysitting every night so he can come to my apartment after Connor goes to bed. Not that I'd want him to anyway. Ben should be able to just be a kid, not the son who watches his sister while his dad has a hookup. That's not right, or okay, and if he was doing that, I wouldn't be as attracted to him as I am.

Thank goodness today I have plans and can't think too much about him and what's going on with him. Riley invited me to a girl's brunch she has once a month with a group of friends she's known forever. She's been my saving grace since I came back to Seattle and moved into this apartment. It doesn't hurt that she's Connor's pediatrician either. Having his doctor live across the hall makes my mommy freak out moments a lot easier to calm.

I swear, without her, I wouldn't go anywhere or make any new friends. All the friends I *used* to have stayed with Seth in Portland, and after being basically deserted by them all once I left him, I'm a little gun shy when it comes to making new ones. I haven't even tried to make friends with any of the other teachers at work for this reason.

A couple have made overtures, but I've rebuffed them, and I probably should change that. I need to make a concerted effort to move past the hurt I felt when Lanie and Sabrina stopped coming around, of course, considering Sabrina is now *dating* my ex-husband, she's no great loss. What kind of *friend* does that anyway? Not a very good one.

The knock on my door startles me out of my dark thoughts and I realize it's time to go and that's probably Riley at the door to tell me to get a move on since I'm riding over with her. Last night was the second Friday sleepover Connor had with my parents, and sleeping in felt *way* too good. I've been dragging since I finally got out of bed.

When the door swings open, it's not Riley standing there. It's *Mitchell*. His in-need-of-a-trim hair falls over his forehead when he grins down at me and I almost melt into a puddle at his feet just by seeing it.

"Hey, Hails." His smile is contagious and I return it, unreasonably happy he's calling me the silly nickname. Most people just call me Hailey and don't bother to shorten it. Seth sure never did. *Hails* would probably make his lip curl in distaste, and that just makes me like it more.

I've never been more suddenly depressed about having to leave than I am right now, but I return his greeting shyly. "Hey."

"Sorry I've been kinda MIA this week," he starts, but he doesn't need to explain.

Waving off his words, I reassure him. "I totally get it. Your kids need to come first. I've been busy with Connor too and figuring out lesson plans for next month, so I probably wouldn't have had a lot of time anyway."

"That may be true, but I'm still sorry. I feel like I've pretty much blown you off this week and that wasn't my intention."

I step closer to put a hand on his arm. My intention is just to squeeze it and let go, but when I touch him, I swear my head gets foggy. His cologne fills my nose and I'm transported back to our date and the way he kissed me. My body sways closer to his, unconsciously wanting to be as close to him as possible, but before his lips meet mine a voice interrupts us.

"Uh, no ma'am. It's not make out with the guy time." Riley's trying to sound stern, but failing miserably because she's giggling by the end of her sentence.

When I look over, she's standing beside me, arms over

her chest, with what I'm sure she thinks is a mean look on her face. My face bursts into flames and Mitchell chuckles. "I wasn't *making out* with anyone."

"You were about to though," is her retort, and she raises one dark eyebrow, waiting for me to try to deny it again.

Mitchell's chuckle turns into an outright laugh and both Riley and I turn our attention to him. He shrugs, turning that smirk on me and making me forget what I was even saying. "She's not wrong. I was about to kiss you."

"Well," Riley informs him, "we don't have time for that. We're meeting friends for brunch, and no boys are allowed." She looks his body up and down, then shakes her head. "No matter how damn hot you are."

"Riley!" I scold her, but she's completely unrepentant.

He looks a little disappointed, but doesn't ask me not to go like Seth would have. Let's be honest, Seth wouldn't have *asked*. He would have just told me I wasn't going and that would've been that. "Call or text me when you get home?" is all Mitchell asks, and I nod. He leans down, dropping a soft kiss to my lips before saying, "Have fun, ladies."

Riley and I both watch him leave. I think we *both* sigh at the sight of his ass in those jeans, something that's proved correct by her next statement. "Damn, I'd like to sink my teeth into that." The visual in my head is of my petite friend with her teeth in Mitchell's backside like a Chihuahua, hanging on for dear life.

Once he's gone, she turns to me and says, "You ready?"

I tell her I am, then follow her out of the apartment and down to her car.

Everyone else is already at the restaurant when we arrive, and they've commandeered two tables to have enough room for everyone. When Riley said "a few friends" I wasn't imagining this many people, and even though I see one person I've met, I sort of want to run away.

Riley doesn't let me do that, holding my hand as she drags me behind her into the bright, open room. My senses are assaulted by the smells of breakfast and by the time we reach their table I'm almost drooling because it smells so damn good.

"Hey y'all," Riley greets everyone, her slight southern accent charming us all.

A pretty brunette stands to hug her. "Hey, sweetie. Glad you could come."

"Me too." Turning to me, she introduces her friend. "Riley, this is Meg Montgomery. She's a nurse I work with at the hospital sometimes." Then, she turns to Meg and continues the intros. "Meg, this is Hailey Lucas—"

She's cut off when Stacey interrupts to say, "Hailey is Sophie's teacher this year." She grins up at me and gives me a finger wave. "Hey, it's good to see you."

"You too." It's nice seeing a friendly face.

Before Riley can continue, she introduces the rest of the group, going around the table in order. "Hailey, meet pretty much all the women in my family. My cousin, Brynna, who's married to Isaac's brother Caleb. Jules, Isaac's sister, and you already met Meg, who's married to one of his other brothers, Will. The only wives missing are Nic, who's married to Matt, and Alecia. She's married to Dominic."

Even though Riley takes her seat right away, I'm staring at Meg in a little of both shock and awe. Hearing that she's married to *Will* when I know as of last week that he's Isaac's brother has me wanting to ask her all sorts of questions. Fangirling over the football player's wife is a little mortifying, but I can't help it.

"Uh, Hailey?" Riley's looking at me like she wants to grab me and force me to sit down beside her but knows it would make things even more awkward if she did that. "What are you doing?" she whispers, "like the rest of the girls can't hear when she has to know they can."

I'm still staring at Meg but manage to shake myself out of my stupor. I feel a little stupid knowing I stood here staring at her for so long, but she gives me an understanding smile. "You're the Hailey that met my husband last weekend, aren't you?" My speech hasn't recovered apparently, so all I can do is nod. "I feel like I should apologize," she laughs. "The man is basically an overgrown child."

"Oops," Riley gives me a sheepish look. "I probably should have warned you who we were meeting."

Now I'm the one giving her a look, but mine says *duh*. "Yeah, Riley, that might have been just a little helpful."

All the women at the table laugh, and the atmosphere in the room changes to one that's way more comfortable than the one I caused by acting like a crazy woman.

Now that the ice has been broken, I take the seat beside Riley, which just happens to be across from Stacey, who winks at me. "Trust me. This family would be a lot to handle even if we didn't have celebrities in it." The rest of them laugh, but I'm so curious.

As much as I want to ask, I don't want to invade their privacy either. Not asking is going to be hard, but being the stalkerish fangirl isn't a good look.

We all place orders, which include plenty of mimosas, and the girls all settle in to talk. I'm amazed at how comfortable they all are with each other. Even the "friends" I had back in Portland weren't this easy to be with. I always felt like they were judging me, while with this group, I feel like I'm just one of the girls and have been here forever.

Meg says my name, and I realize it's not the first time. "What's it like having Sophie for so many hours a day?" She grins over at Stacey, clearly teasing her. "That child has a mind of her own."

"She gets that from her father," Stacey tells us all, and we all laugh.

Brynna leans over to bump Stacey with her shoulder. "I don't think it's all from Isaac. Seems like I remember you being the exact same way when you were that age."

"I have no idea what you're talking about." Stacey can't even keep a straight face when she says this, and Brynna dissolves into giggles with her. Once they've sobered, she turns to me. "Oh, Hailey, I wanted to ask you. Sophie is having a dance recital in a few weeks and she would love for you to come watch. I think there are a couple of kids from her class who are dancing, and I know having you show up to surprise them would just make their day. I know Sophie talks about you all the time."

Her words bring an uncontrollable smile to my lips. I

love hearing that my kids like me, and Sophie's such a sweet child. "Oh, I'd love to! Thank you so much for inviting me." Taking out my phone, I put the date and time into my calendar and save it so I won't forget.

"Yay! I'm so glad." Stacey smiles at me warmly. "Sophie will love showing her moves off to someone new. I think she's bored with all of us now. We aren't the best audience since we've seen it all."

Them talking about other students in the class being part of the recital makes me wonder if Evie is in it too, but I don't want to ask and call attention to the fact that I'm sort of dating her dad. I'm still a little wary of people finding out and am just counting myself lucky that we didn't run into anyone I had to worry about on our date aside from Isaac.

Once she's gotten my agreement, Stacey's attention turns back to her sisters-in-law and the conversation turns to husbands and kids and what everyone is planning to do this weekend. I'm glad the focus is off me and when the waitress brings our food I settle in to eat. It's all so good. I'll have to remember this place.

After brunch and on the way home, I ask Riley, "Why didn't you warn me we'd be having brunch with Will Montgomery's wife and most of his family?"

She laughs. "Sorry, honey. I didn't think about it. I've met up with them a few times now and it doesn't faze me the way it used to. Plus, Will is just the tip of the iceberg. The recital they were talking about? The two teachers used to work with *Starla*. Can you believe that?" I don't get to say anything before she drops a major bomb on me. "And one of them, not one who was there today, but one of them is married to *Luke Williams*. Trust me, I almost passed out when I found out. It was all I could do not to grill the poor woman on what it was like to be married to him."

"Wow," is all I can think to say. Luke Williams was the guy *every* girl had a crush on back when he did those vampire movies. I am *not* ashamed to say I had posters of him on every wall and just might have written "Hailey Williams" on more than one notebook.

"Mmhmm. And his wife is gorgeous and sweet too. They're both way more down to earth than you would think."

I wonder if she's the pediatrician for any of these famous families, but I don't ask. It feels like that would be invading their privacy, and hers too.

Riley continues to chatter the rest of the way home and I just enjoy hanging out with someone who isn't under ten. She's so much fun, and meeting her has definitely been one of the highlights of moving back home. It's nice to have a genuine friend, and she's such a sweet person. I'm sure her patients love her, even when she has to give them shots. I know Connor sure does. He's fascinated with her red hair.

We pull into the parking lot and I send a text to my mom to let her know I'm home so she can bring Connor. She replies quickly to say she'll be here shortly, and we aren't even at our stairs when I see Mitchell with his Evie at the playground. I freeze, watching him laugh as he chases his daughter around the play area. She's shrieking with glee, and the site brings a smile to my face.

"Go talk to him," Riley urges. "You deserve someone who looks at you the way he does."

Her words are so sweet, I can't help but reach forward to hug her. "Thanks. I'll talk to you later?"

"Of course. Go get 'em, tiger."

CHAPTER 21

Mitchell

I know it's the kid who's supposed to get worn out playing, but after an hour of chasing Evie around the playground acting like I'm the Beast from her favorite movie I'm ready for a nap.

"Mrs. Lucas!" she screams before taking off running for the edge of the play area.

Hailey's just stepping onto the rubber material when Evie slams into her, wrapping her arms around her waist and beaming up at her. I watch Hailey look down at her, her face softening as she smiles down at my daughter and runs a hand down her hair. Whatever she says has Evie's grin widening in a way that seems like it should be impossible.

After their short conversation, Evie releases Hailey so she can grab her by the hand and pull her over to where she left me. "Look, Daddy, it's Mrs. Lucas." Hearing her call her *Mrs.* has me clenching my fists because she feels like she's *mine*. She's certainly not *his* anymore. *Dumbass.*

"Hey," she greets me shyly, not quite looking me in the eye.

Evie keeps pulling her closer until she's standing so close our chests almost touch when we breathe. "Can she play with us, Daddy?"

"I don't know, Evie. Ms. Lucas might have things she needs to do today. You already see her just about every day anyway." I'm hoping she agrees to stick around, at least for a few minutes. I want to be around her, to breathe her in, even if it's just for a few minutes.

Her head lifts, but her attention is more on Evie than me. "I can for a few minutes." She looks down at her phone and twists her lips to one side. "My mom will be bringing my little boy home soon."

This excites Evie even more. "Awesome!" she squeals, bouncing up and down on her toes. "I can play with him *and* you." She's so excited she can't contain herself and she starts running around in circles around us.

Hailey covers her mouth so her giggles aren't obvious and I want to pull her into my embrace when I see her eyes sparkling with mirth. Even though I know I shouldn't, once I'm sure Evie has gone back to the swings I lean forward and whisper in her ear, "I'd like to play with you too." It's more forward than I've been up to this point. A week without being able to touch her or even have a real conversation with her has me desperate to stake my claim before someone else tries to.

Red crawls from the top of her chest up to her cheeks

and seeing her blush at my words makes my dick twitch in my jeans. If it wasn't for Evie and Ben, plus her mom coming with her son soon, I'd drag her up to my apartment and show her just how that blush makes me feel.

"Mitch," she hisses, and I think it might be the first time she's shortened my name into a nickname. It makes me happier than is sane, but I grin down at her anyway. "There are *children* nearby." Her eyes dart around the almost empty playground guiltily, like she's afraid someone might have heard me say dirty things to her. She's too adorable for words.

Now I do step closer and pull her into my side. It makes speaking directly into her ear easier. And, it has the added benefits of allowing me to both touch *and* smell her. "I've missed you this week, Hails. It's been hard not being able to come see you or talk to you very much. A couple of minutes when I'm picking up Evie and Ben just doesn't cut it."

The smile she gives me after telling her this makes the fact that saying it at all has me feeling like the biggest pussy easier to swallow. "You're so sweet." She relaxes further into my side and I hold her tighter.

"Only with you." Yeah, I'll admit, it sounds like a line, but it's not. I gave up trying to be sweet to Tabitha long before our marriage finally ended. Being this way with Hailey is natural though.

I want to hold her longer, but she moves away from me when a car pulls into the lot. It must be her mom with her boy. Watching as she runs across to greet them, I can't help but wish Tab was like that with our kids. Instead, she acts like they're an inconvenience, only to be trotted out when they can benefit her in some way. It's about the same way she treated me, though at least with me, she had some use for me or we wouldn't even *have* the two kids. And that would be a tragedy.

Hailey's quick to get her son out of the car and after saying what I'm sure is goodbye to her mom, she walks with him over to us. She's holding him instead of letting him walk, and I can see him squirming to be released. Evie waits impatiently for them to step back up onto the rubber mats that make up the playground floor, but as soon as Hailey puts her son down, she runs right over to introduce herself.

I walk over too, after giving Hailey a minute to get Evie and Connor acquainted and when she sees me, Evie smiles brightly. "Look, Daddy. Isn't he cute?"

"He is," I tell her, crouching down so I'm eye level with her and closer to Connor. He looks up at me like I'm an interesting object he doesn't understand, sticking his fingers in his mouth and grinning toothily up at me.

It seems like it's been so long since my kids were this age, but Evie's not quite nine so it's not been that long. Shaking off the melancholy feeling that knowledge gives me, I hold out a hand for him to shake and he tilts his head to one side and just looks at it.

"Daddy," Evie giggles, "he doesn't know how to shake." Taking the hand that isn't stuffed in his mouth; she puts it in mine and tells him, "This is how you do it. Shake, shake, shake." She says the word every time she makes our hands move up and down and he chortles in glee, loving every moment of the attention.

Connor takes his other hand out of his mouth and

starts patting our joined hands with it. Evie jerks her hand away at the wet feel, saying "Gross! Ew, Connor," while Hailey gasps and rushes forward to pick him up.

"I'm so sorry." He transfers his wet patting to her and she's looking down at me with so much mortification she doesn't even notice.

Standing from my crouching position, I put my hand on her shoulder and try to reassure her. "It's fine. I have two kids, so I'm used to feeling all kinds of drooled on things." I smile, hoping to relax her, and it works. Her stiff spine relaxes a bit and she grins up at me. "Now, why don't we let the kids play and you and I can talk." She looks unsure, but Evie is way too happy to take Connor off her hands.

"Please, Mrs. Lucas? I promise I'll watch him." Evie has her hands clasped under her chin the way she always does when she's begging. She thinks the position, with the big wide eyes and pouty lips, will get her anything she wants, and truthfully, she's not wrong. I haven't been able to resist her yet.

Hailey considers her for a few more minutes before relenting. "Okay, for a few minutes. Don't let him climb up high."

Evie rolls her eyes. "I knoooow." The attitude on this kid, I swear. Grabbing Connor by the hand, she says, "Let's go play," in a voice about three octaves higher than her normal voice.

Once she's out of earshot, I turn to Hailey. "That attitude comes from her mother, not me."

"Uh-huh." It sounds like she's agreeing, but based on

the raised eyebrow I think she's more than a little disbelieving.

"It's true. Tabitha is *all* attitude, all the time. It's exhausting." Talking to the person you're trying to get close to about your ex is probably the worst thing to do, but she needs to know how things with my ex are and how she is if she's going to be a part of my life.

Hailey ignores my attempts to convince her and turns her attention back to where the kids are climbing the steps to the low platform. There's a slide there that's not too far off the ground and I'm betting that's where Evie's going to take Connor.

She's walking behind him, arms outstretched around him like she's trying to shield and I have to laugh at the way she's hunched over. All of her focus on him. She doesn't even care that I'm laughing at the spectacle she's making.

As soon as Connor's seated at the top of the slide, Evie starts talking to him, gesturing with her hands like she's telling him to stay as though he's her pet. I'm sure he has no idea what she wants him to do, but amazingly enough, he sits still long enough for her to run down and around to the bottom of the slide so she can catch him.

Hailey's focus is all on Connor as she watches him and Evie like a hawk. Her attentiveness to her son only makes her more attractive. My thoughts become words before I think about the consequences, startling us both. "Have dinner with us."

"What?" Her eyes are comically wide when she turns to look at me.

I'm uncharacteristically embarrassed by the way I just word vomited that out at her but own it anyway. "Have dinner with us." She starts to say something, so I hurry to explain before she turns me down flat. "I've missed you this week, Hails." Her face softens at my admission and a smile tips up one side of her lips. "It's been busy, and we've only had a couple of phone calls and greetings when the kids are getting picked up. I want more than that with you."

A pretty flush covers her cheeks. "I want more with you too."

"Good. Then eat with us. It won't be anything fancy, but I promise it won't kill you either."

I wink, and she laughs. "Okay, but only because you promised. Can I bring anything?"

"Just yourself."

Biting down on her bottom lip, she's suddenly apprehensive. "But…"

I want to know what she's thinking, but I hope whatever it is doesn't deter her from coming over. Getting to spend time with her, to build the relationship I want to have, is hard when we both have jobs and children to take care of. "But… what?"

"What are your kids going to think?"

She sounds genuinely worried, but she doesn't have any reason to. "They're going to think we have company for dinner." Maybe I'm being deliberately obtuse, but why would they care if she comes over for dinner?

The scathing look she gives me would scald all the skin off my body if it was possible. "Oh, do you have women over for dinner so much they won't even notice? If that's the case, I think I'll pass."

Now she's the one being ridiculous. "No, that's not what I meant. Hailey," I sigh, running a hand through my too-long hair. "It's not like me being on a date would be detrimental to them, and you're not some stranger either." I'm not explaining this right. I know I'm not, but I don't know how to make her understand. "I want a relationship with you."

"I want that too."

Well, that's good to hear. "Good. But, in order to have that relationship, we have to spend time together. Both alone and with our kids. We can't have any kind of relationship if they aren't involved at all." Laying it out in a way I know she won't misunderstand or misconstrue, I tell her, "I'm not looking for a hookup."

Hailey sighs. "I'm not either, Mitchell, but I don't want to upset your children. You haven't been divorced that long, and kids don't understand grown-up situations."

"That's true, but Hailey, you have to remember, Tabitha and I weren't together for a while before we made it legal. The kids are used to seeing us as separate. I promise you have nothing to worry about."

She still looks unsure, but she finally agrees to come and I send up a prayer of thanks. I need her to see just how good we can be together.

CHAPTER 22

Hailey

I'm nervous about going to Mitchell's for dinner. I don't think he even considered what his kids would think about me showing up. Evie, I'm sure will be thrilled that her teacher is there, but Ben is older, and I'm sure seeing his dad with someone who isn't his mom won't be easy for him.

No matter how many times Mitchell tried to convince me it was fine, I can't bring myself to believe it. It can't be that easy.

It's time for us to head over and Connor is excited to go see Evie again. I'm pretty sure he has a little crush on her after playing with her this afternoon. Playing with other kids is his favorite thing to do, and makes me regret sometimes not having a little brother or sister for him to play with. With the way things ended, it's better that we didn't. Being the single parent of one child is hard enough. I don't know how Mitchell does it with two, though he does have some help from his ex.

We're just about to leave for Mitchell's when my cell phone rings. Connor's trying to get out the front door, so I don't look before I answer. "Hello?"

The voice on the other end makes my blood run cold. "Hello, Hailey."

I can't say anything at first. My mouth opens, closes, and then does it again. Swallowing hard I try to get rid of the sudden lump in my throat before croaking out his name. "*Seth?*" My head is reeling because there aren't very many reasons for him to be calling me. I haven't heard from him since the day our divorce became final. After a few seconds spent internally freaking out, I finally manage to ask, "What do you want?"

"Am I interrupting something?" I can imagine the way he's looking at the phone, one eyebrow raised with a scowl on his face because I'm not jumping to do whatever it is he wants.

"Not interrupting, but I have somewhere to be soon so I need to get moving." I struggle to keep my temper in check. The way he acts like *I'm* inconveniencing *him* by not wanting to talk pisses me off. He hasn't had time for me in *months*, and now that he's decided he wants to talk I'm supposed to abandon any plans I might have.

Seth sighs, sounding extremely put out. My eyes roll skyward as I pray for patience. "I'll make this quick then." The tone of his voice is the snotty one he uses when he's speaking to someone he considers to be beneath him and man does it make me want to kick him in a very sensitive place.

"That would be great." I hope my sarcasm is as clear to him as it is to me.

"I've moved back to Seattle."

He drops this bomb on me like it's nothing. I begged for *years* to move back, especially after I got pregnant with Connor and he said our lives were in Portland and he would never move back. Now, suddenly he's *here*?

"You moved back? When?"

Huffing out an irritated breath, he tells me, "Two months ago."

I have to bite down on the inside of my cheek to keep from screaming. Two months and I'm just now finding out?

My inner rant is cut off when he drops his next bomb. "I'd like to see Connor."

"What?" This conversation is not making me sound very intelligent. All I'm doing is parroting back what he says and saying *what*. Oddly, I do get a little satisfaction from it, but only because it drives Seth crazy when someone repeats everything he says.

He's annoyed now. "I want to see Connor."

"Why now? You haven't wanted anything to do with him in a year."

Seth is quiet for a while, so long I pull the phone away from my ear to make sure we're still connected. Finally, he asks, "Does it matter? I'm his father and I have the right to see him."

"You're right," I say slowly, "you do, but up until now,

you haven't taken advantage of those rights. I just want to know what changed."

He sighs again, like I'm asking something totally unreasonable. "When can I see him?"

Oh, okay, so that's the game we're playing now. I'm going to ask questions and he's going to refuse to answer them. Sure, why not. "I don't know Seth. What does your schedule look like? I'm at work until about four every weekday, so it would have to be after that." I want to tell him no, he can't see Connor, but our custody agreement says he can. He just hasn't taken advantage of it.

"Why not tonight?"

Yup, here we go. Now I'm struggling to keep my temper in check so he doesn't know he's ticking me off. If he knows I'm angry, he wins. "I already have plans tonight. You know that because I already *told* you that."

"So you're denying me the chance to see my child?"

"No, Seth, that's not what I'm doing at all. You can't expect to call me and have me drop everything to meet you when you haven't bothered to call to check on Connor or try to see him since the day our divorce was final. If you want to see him so soon, we can meet tomorrow if you want." Honestly, it's more than he should hope for because I could adhere to the custody agreement that says he's allowed to have him one overnight during the week and one weekend a month because his lawyer said his schedule was "too booked" to do every other weekend. *Jackass.*

A few minutes of silence follow my attempt at being civil, then he says, "I'm busy tomorrow, so it will have to be next weekend if you can't make time for me to see my son today."

I'm rolling my eyes so much they're going to get stuck in a weird position. "It's not about 'making time' Seth, it's about having plans already. You can't expect to call me at the last minute assuming I don't have anything better to do than come meet you. If you want to set something up for next weekend, text me your schedule and I'll let you know when I'm available too." I know he's going to have something to say that will ruin my night more than he already has, so I rush to end the call. "Now, if you'll excuse me, I need to get going. Bye, Seth."

There's no "bye" in return. Seth just disconnects the call and I pull my phone away from my ear to stare down at it. I hope I don't regret what just happened. If Seth decides to take me to court, I won't be able to afford the type of lawyer he'll get. Maybe if he paid the alimony and child support that he's supposed to, but it's been sporadic and never the amount it should be.

Looking down at Connor, who's playing on the floor with a couple of his trucks, I hold out a hand. "You ready to go, sweetie?"

Blue eyes that match his father's look up at me and he grabs my hand, using it to pull himself up to standing. Once he's steady, we leave for Mitchell's apartment.

Dinner goes well... I guess? I don't really remember. As much as I hate to admit it, I wasn't fully present all night, and I'm sure I made a very crappy impression. All I could think about was Seth wanting to be part of Connor's life after so long. I guess a year isn't *that* long, but if, heaven forbid, Connor didn't live with me? I'd see him every single chance I could. Seth not wanting to be bothered is something I just don't understand.

Back in the apartment for the night, I get Connor ready for bed, doing only the bare minimum because after spending all evening playing with Evie and Ben, he's so tired he's almost falling asleep in the tub. I wouldn't even bother with a bath, but I think he wore more mashed potatoes than he put into his mouth.

As soon as he's in his pajamas, I take him back to his room. We sit in the glider beside his toddler bed and rock as I read his current favorite book, but he doesn't last more than a few pages before he's snoring lightly. I smile down at him, running my finger down his soft little cheek. The love I feel for him isn't something I can put into words. It's just there and infinite. Never-ending and true.

I'm just pulling the door to his room shut when there's a loud knock on my door. My first thought is *Seth*. Is he showing up hoping to have time with Connor? Who else would be coming here so late at night?

Checking the peephole is something I know I should do, but I'm so panicked I bypass it completely. The door opens, but it's not Seth on the other side... it's Mitchell.

CHAPTER 23

Mitchell

*H*ailey was preoccupied all night. She missed things the kids said to her, picked at her food, and basically ignored me. Ben watched her closely all night, and I know he wasn't impressed. I didn't need him to tell me, but he didn't wait long after the door shut to tell me I needed to cut her loose and find someone better. Someone who is good with him and Evie. The funny thing is, she *was* and *is* good with Evie. I'm not sure what happened tonight.

It kills me to wait until Evie's in bed, but as soon as she is, I head for Hailey's apartment, telling Ben to keep an eye on his sister until I return. It probably makes me an awful parent to leave my thirteen-year-old in charge of my sleeping eight-year-old, but I'm not going very far and he has my number if anything happens.

My fist pounds on her door much harder than I plan, but I own it. I need to talk to her, to find out what happened to her between the playground and dinner. I don't think it was just the stress of eating dinner with my kids either, so she better not give me that shit.

She opens the door and I watch as her body relaxes the moment she realizes it's me at her door.

"Who were you expecting?"

Hailey blinks up at me, a little lost. "Huh?"

"Just now. Who were you expecting to be at your door? And, why didn't you check your peephole."

Her spine goes rigid and she draws herself up to her full height. "That's none of your business, and how do you know I didn't?

"C'mon, Hailey. I'm not stupid. If you'd checked the peephole, you wouldn't have been shocked to see me instead of whoever else you were expecting. Who was it?" Jealousy explodes in my veins, making my voice harsher than I intend, but fuck it.

She still swears she wasn't expecting anyone, and it pisses me the fuck off. Instead of standing here in the hallway arguing with her, I push my way inside her apartment. Hailey probably thinks I'm a dick for doing it, but at the moment I don't care. Depending on how this conversation goes, I'll probably regret it later.

"What are you doing?" she asks incredulously. "You do know you're supposed to *wait* to be invited inside someone's house, right?"

I cross my arms over my chest and just stare at her, saying nothing. I'm not about to defend myself to someone who won't even tell me the truth. "Who were you expecting to be at the door Hailey?"

She shuts the door with a groan and turns back to face me. "It. Doesn't. Matter." The words are said through clenched teeth, but I don't let it phase me.

"It damn well does matter, Hailey. Especially if whoever you were expecting to be at the door is also the reason you were so out of it tonight." I'm not about to beg her for information, but one way or another she will tell me what's going on.

Hailey shakes her head stubbornly, refusing to admit anything.

"Who was it?" I take a step toward her, waiting for her to tell me.

"Like I said, it doesn't matter." Her chin lifts, and she stares up at me in defiance. God, it's such a turn on that she stands up to me.

Taking another step forward, I ask again. "Who. Was. It?" Again she tells me it doesn't matter and we continue this dance until I'm standing so close to her our chests touch with every angry breath we take.

Finally, she breaks, throwing her hands in the air in frustration and forcing me to step back so they don't hit me. "Oh my *God*, fine. If you want to know so badly, I'll tell you." Her eyes are practically spitting fire at me. "*Seth*." His name is said like a curse.

"Why did you think Seth would be at your door?" I'm confused because she said he still lives in Portland. He'd have to drive all the way down here just to show up at her door. Why would he do that?

Hailey curls into herself, her back resting against the

door. She looks so sad I want to reach out and pull her into my arms, but I don't think she'll accept my comfort right now. "He's moved back to Seattle."

My body tenses to the point it feels like my skin is stretched taut. "What? When? What does he want?" I spit the questions at her and she flinches when each one lands.

"He says he wants to see Connor. Seth wanted me to let him see him tonight and wasn't very happy when I told him I already had plans."

She looks down, all the color draining out of her face at this confession. That's what it feels like, like she's confessing her sins to me, when it's nothing of the sort. "Okay, and what happened after that?" I ask when she doesn't continue.

Hailey shrugs. "He wants to see him next weekend, so I told him to text me when he'll be available and I'll let him know."

"*Fuck that.*" My hands clench into fists at my sides. After the shitty way he treated her, the fucked up way he treats his *kid*, now he wants to see him? I call bullshit. "You're not going to see him alone."

Her gaze lifts from where she was staring at the floor to glare at me. "Excuse me? You don't get to tell me what to do, Mitchell. We've had one date, two if you count dinner tonight. That does *not* give you the right to make decisions for me."

"Whoa, hold on a second." I hold both hands up in front of my body and try to reason with her. "I'm not trying to tell you what to do. I'm just saying if you're going, I am too. He's a jackass and if he tries to pull something I don't want you to have to deal with him alone."

She's already shaking her head when I finish. "You being there will just make things worse."

"No, me being there means *he* can't make things worse. Big difference."

Hailey rubs her forehead with a hand like she's getting a migraine. I should feel bad for causing her more stress, but I don't. She can be mad at me all she wants, but she'll be mad while I'm standing there beside her so the dickhead can't mess with her.

She finally lowers her hand, but her shoulders slump, making her look defeated. I can't handle her looking that way without trying to do something to fix it. Cupping her cheeks in my hands, I lift her face so she's forced to meet my eyes.

Tears fill her eyes, in serious danger of falling and something in my chest squeezes at the sight of her pain. "Baby," I murmur, dropping my hands so I can pull her into my arms. Her head comes to rest on my shoulder and when I kiss the top of her head she starts to cry. Hailey's body is wracked with sobs and I hate the thought that I might be responsible for some of them.

Lifting her up, I cradle her ass with my hands and she wraps her legs around me. I walk over to the couch and sit down, leaving her no choice but to straddle my lap. Her head is still on my shoulder, her hands clutching my shirt to pull herself as close to me as she can. Rubbing my hand up and down her back I try to soothe her, murmuring what I hope are comforting words.

After a few minutes, her crying quiets until all that's left is shuddering breaths and the occasional hiccup. Hailey eventually sits up to look at me and even with tear tracks on her cheeks and red, swollen eyes, she's the most beautiful woman I've ever seen.

I start to speak, to say her name, but her lips crash down on mine. Any thoughts of speech are forgotten. I've spent the last week dreaming of Hailey's lips on mine, and even though I know I shouldn't take advantage of her when she's just been crying, I don't want to hurt her either.

Hailey pulls back to trace the seam of my lips with her tongue, trying to control our kiss, and I take over. Wrapping her long hair around my fist, I use my hold to tilt her head the way I want it and push my tongue into her mouth.

She moans at the first touch of our tongues but doesn't hesitate to stroke mine with hers. The feeling has me groaning into her mouth while she whimpers into mine. Our kiss goes on forever, our heads tilting first one way, then the other, and the more she gets into it, the more restless Hailey gets.

A few minutes after we start devouring each other, her hips start to rock on my lap, and even through her panties, I can feel how hot she is. I'm instantly glad she's wearing a dress because *goddamn*, I want to feel all of her more than I want my next breath.

Her movements are jerky, so I grip her waist with my free hand to guide her movements. Her pussy slides against my cock and I almost come in my jeans like a teenager at the feel of it. She feels so damn good, even with three layers of clothes separating us.

"Mitchell," she whimpers my name as her thighs tighten against my legs. Already she's close to coming, which tells me it's been a minute since another man has touched her.

Hell, just that thought makes my hand tighten on her waist because she's choosing to let *me* be the one who touches her. I don't deserve it, but I'm damn sure going to take it.

I run my hand up her side slowly, stopping just under the swell of her breast. Her spine straightens, pushing her flesh closer to me in invitation, so I take what she's offering by brushing my thumb across her nipple. It's obvious she's as turned on as I am.

Her mouth leaves mine when I touch her and her breath catches. Our eyes meet for a second, then she drops her head to my shoulder where I can feel her panting against my neck.

Releasing my hold on her hair, I bring both hands up to cover her breasts, squeezing gently with my palms, then using my fingers to pinch the tight nubs. Every move I make has her hips moving against me faster and her breaths turn into constant whimpers the closer she gets to her climax.

I want more than anything to put my hand in her panties before she comes, but I don't know if she'll let me. To test the waters, I slide one hand down her belly, stopping at the apex of her thighs to give her a chance to say no.

"Please." It's a breathy plea, barely enough sound to be heard, but my ears are attuned to every noise she makes.

My hand moves slowly, pulling up the hem of her dress one inch at a time until I can look down and see her silky lavender panties. They're almost the exact same color as the dress she's wearing and I wonder if her bra matches too. I don't wonder for long though, I'm way more interested in what's *inside* her panties.

Stroking my finger along the center of her panties, I have to force myself not to go too fast. Even through the silk covering her, she's soft and warm. I want my hands all over her. My next pass over her, I press a little harder and feel the rise of her clit under my fingertip. The rougher touch has her moaning against my throat, then she presses her lips against my skin and sucks lightly.

My excitement rises at her response and I carefully pull the edge of her panties over to the other side so I can see what I'm doing to her pussy. Just looking at her does something to me. She's so pretty and pink... and so goddamn *wet*. I want to make her *drenched*, make her *messy*. It's a feeling I've never had before and one that's a little shocking, honestly.

Instead of going right for her pussy now that it's bared to my gaze, I stroke my hand up and down her thigh, enjoying the goosebumps that raise in my wake. Hailey starts to squirm harder against me and muttering words I don't understand. They sound a little desperate, like she's close to begging me to touch her, so I stop teasing her.

The first touch of my finger on her slick flesh makes her moan loudly, the inside of her thighs quivering against mine as I stroke her. Her pussy is clean-shaven and her clit is a hard little knot that's dying for my attention.

"Mitchell, please," Hailey moans. Her head lifts, the lust in her eyes crystal clear. Keeping my eyes on her, I run my finger around her clit, careful not to touch it at first, before pinching it between my fingers.

Her whole body trembles against me as she erupts in orgasm. Her eyes close and she throws her head back, beautiful in her release. It takes everything I have not to come myself. I wanted this to be all about her because I'm guessing that hasn't happened to her very often. From what she's said about her ex, he's a selfish bastard who probably didn't make sure she came at all.

Hailey's attention slowly focuses back on me and she looks well-pleasured with her eyes at half-mast and a pretty blush on her face. Her lips are puffy, both from my kisses and her biting them. As I watch, her blush deepens. She's starting to realize where she is and what I just did to her and I can see the lust turn to embarrassment before my eyes.

"Baby," I start, but she tenses at my voice and looks away. Grabbing her waist with both hands, I snap, "Hailey." I shouldn't be so hard when I say her name, but I can see her starting to panic which is the last thing I want.

Saying her name that way gets her attention and she turns back to face me. I lean in and press a soft kiss to first her top lip, then her bottom, before kissing the tip of her nose and finally both her closed eyelids. She relaxes in my hold with each small kiss, and when her eyes open, they look less troubled.

"Hey," I say softly, not wanting to scare her off again. "What we just did? It was the best moment of my day... maybe even my year."

Her eyes fill with tears and I worry for a second that I said something wrong, but she wraps her arms around my neck and hugs me to her. My hands go around her waist and I pull her in as close as I can, enjoying just holding her against me.

We sit like this for a few minutes, but all too soon I have to break the connection. Hailey sits up straight to look at me, and as much as I hate to do it, I tell her, "I should probably get home. Ben's with Evie, but I didn't plan to stay as long as I have."

She nods, climbing from my lap and standing in front of me with one arm wrapped around her stomach like she's trying to protect herself. The pose is defensive and makes me run what I just said through my head again. *Shit*. That did *not* come out the way I meant it.

"Hey," I tell her, pulling her arm free with one hand and putting the other under her chin to make her look at me. I don't want there to be any confusion. "I meant what I said, Hailey. Leaving you right now is the last thing I want to do, but I can't leave Ben there all night with Evie. They aren't old enough for that."

Her eyes narrow and she pulls her face away from my hand. "I know that, Mitchell."

"Then what was with the..." I trail off and wave my hand near her stomach "...that."

Rolling her eyes heavenward, she sighs heavily before explaining. "Just because I know *why* you have to leave doesn't make it any less awkward. This—" now she's the one doing the gesturing, from my body to hers "—wasn't something I planned on happening tonight and now that it has, I don't know how to act around you."

I can see that telling me that embarrassed her even

149

further, especially when she mutters, "And I'm so glad you just made me explain."

"So, we're good then?"

The looks she gives me is glacial. "Yes, Mitchell, we're 'good.'" This is said complete with finger quotes, which should tell me she doesn't mean it, but she's already said she does, and I don't want to question her again.

Stepping forward, I wrap an arm around her waist and pull her into my embrace. I lean forward, stopping with my lips barely touching hers to say, "Good," one last time before I kiss her one last time.

After we break apart, I kiss her forehead, then take her hand and lead her to her front door. "I'll text you later?"

Hailey nods, and once I'm through the door she shuts it behind me. I wait to hear her twist the deadbolt before walking away, my head replaying what happened and wishing I didn't have to leave right after. One time, I swear we'll be able to finish this, and I'll be able to stay all damn night. Once with her won't be enough, I already know that.

Ben's sitting on the couch playing a game when I walk back into our apartment and doesn't even look up when I come in. I drop down beside him, reaching over to hit the button to pause on his controller and wait for him to complain. Surprisingly, he doesn't.

He barely turns, looking at me out of the corner of his eye. "Everything okay?"

As much as I know it will irritate him, I mess up the hair on his head before saying, "Yeah, I think so. Connor's dad wants to see him, even though it's been over a year. Since you and Evie will be with your mom, I'm going to

go with Hailey, so she isn't alone with him. He's a dick."
Fuck. I'm supposed to watch my mouth around the kids,
but I suck at it. It's not like they don't hear the words all
the time anyway, especially Ben, but Tabitha will be pissed
if he repeats my words.

"Alright bud," I look up at the clock and realize it's way
past his bedtime. "You need to get in the shower and get
in bed."

Ben groans, but doesn't argue, so I'm left sitting on the
couch and staring at the blank television with my
thoughts.

CHAPTER 24

Hailey

I've spent all week dreaming about the night Mitchell followed me back to my apartment to find out what was bothering me. The only thing about my dreams? They don't end with Mitchell leaving after putting his hand in my panties. No, these end in my bedroom when he's laid me down on my bed and started taking his clothes off.

I always wake up right before his pants come off. It's so depressing... and sexually frustrating. I'm in danger of wearing out my vibrator. Good thing it's one of those ones that has a cord and is rechargeable otherwise I'd probably be broke.

Today is just one more morning where I wake up hot and bothered, but unlike every other morning, I don't have time to take care of my problem. I'm supposed to meet Seth at ten-thirty because he's evil and believes in meeting early in the day on a freaking Saturday, probably just to inconvenience me further.

I didn't tell him about Mitchell coming with me. Maybe I should've, but I don't really think he'll care very much. He might be bothered by Mitchell knowing he's a shitty father, but not because he cares about his parenting skills. Seth is just way too focused on his image and what people think about him. You'd think that would mean he'd put forth an effort with our son so people would praise him, but he hasn't thus far. I'll honestly be shocked if he actually shows up this morning. It would be just like him to make the plans, force me to get myself and Connor up, ready, and out the door so early just to stand me up.

Getting Connor up, dressed and fed before we have to leave is an ordeal. If we didn't have somewhere to go, the kid would have been up at six and wanting to play. Because I need him up and pleasant, he fought me on getting up and then screamed the whole time he was getting dressed. He didn't want to wear the clothes I picked out, and after trying to force his stiff limbs into the shirt and jeans I pulled out of his drawers, I let him pick his own.

Talk about regret. Connor clearly wants his dad to think I'm color-blind and homeless. The shirt he insists on wearing has a rip near the hem and stains I'm afraid to even attempt to identify. For pants, he's wearing a pair of sweats that are almost too small for him, so I let him stay in just his underwear until breakfast is finished. I'm hoping he'll let me put real clothes on him before we leave because there's no way I'm showing up for the first visit with his father in a year with him looking like I can't afford to buy clothes for him.

After breakfast, he finally does let me put better clothes on him, but that might have something to do with the fact that while he was eating a waffle and banana slices I hid what he was trying to wear.

By the time we're both finally ready to go I want to take a nap, but that's not an option I have available. Besides, Mitchell is coming over to ride with us, and he shows up right as I'm debating on going back to bed and pretending today isn't happening.

"Hey," he greets me when I open the door. He's cleaned up his beard since I saw him the other day when he dropped Evie off at school. It's a good look on him and makes me want to see if it's still as soft as it was when he was kissing me last weekend. Thoughts I shouldn't be having right before meeting up with Seth.

Grabbing Connor's hand after I return his hello, we follow him out to my car where he holds out a hand for my keys. I look up at him in question because it's *my* car we're taking today, not his, since mine has Connor's seat in it already.

"I'm driving."

Oh Lord, here we go. "Uh, no, you're not. My car, I'm driving."

Mitchell shakes his head and gives me a look like he feels sorry for me. "Sorry, Hails, but I'm not riding shot-gun... *ever.*"

Of all the chauvinist... "Why?" I'm not sure why I ask the question because I'm sure I already know the answer. "That's such a guy way to be."

"Uh, sweetheart?" He runs a hand along his front. "In case you haven't noticed, I *am* a guy."

I wave him off. "Whatever. Just because you're a man doesn't mean you can't be a passenger in a car."

He huffs out a laugh before smirking over at me. "I know that. But, still, I'm driving."

"Fine." I hand over the keys even though I'd prefer to throw them right at his smug face. Once Connor is secured in his seat with his favorite two trucks, I get in on the passenger side, still grumbling about men and their inability to be reasonable. Mitchell ignores me of course, so I choose the radio station before he gets a chance to. "If you get to drive, I get to pick what we listen to." His smirk turns into a grimace when I turn on the station playing the most bubblegum pop music I know of.

The ride to the park where we're meeting Seth goes by way too quickly, and before I'm ready, we're pulling into the parking lot where I can see his car already waiting. When I look down at my watch, I can see we're ten minutes early, but because he was here first, he'll probably still complain we're late. And then there's the fit he's likely to throw when he sees Mitchell with me. Seth is the king of *I don't want her, but you can't have her*, so I just know he's going to show his ass.

He's still sitting in his car when we pull up beside him to park and he doesn't look our way, probably because Mitchell backs into the spot so he's between us. I won't deny I *love* him doing that. He's putting himself in the middle like a buffer and protecting me from whatever bullshit my ex-husband decides to spew.

To get this meeting over with, I go ahead and get out

of the car so I can let Connor out. By the time I set Connor on the ground, Mitchell's beside me, taking the diaper bag out of my hand and carrying it himself. He also puts his hand in the small of my back when we start walking around the car to greet Seth, making it clear we're a team.

Seth doesn't get out of his car until we come back around to the area between the two vehicles. When he does, he looks Mitchell up and down with a disgusted sneer on his face.

The two men couldn't be more different. Seth's wearing a pair of light khaki pants, the last thing he should be wearing to chase a toddler around a *park*, paired with a pale blue polo shirt that I'm sure he picked because it matches the color of his eyes. His blonde hair is styled neatly, not a single hair out of place.

In contrast, Mitchell's wearing a pair of faded, ripped jeans, the kind destroyed by lots of washes... *not* because he bought them that way the way Seth would. His shirt has the Harley Davidson logo on it and barely contains his muscular arms, and while his beard may be cleaned up, he still has it. His deep brown hair is just a shade too long and messy like he ran his hands through it while it was still wet but didn't bother to even attempt to tame it.

Mitchell is the opposite of Seth in every way and until this moment I didn't really notice. Not because it isn't obvious, but because I've had other things on my mind than the differences between them.

The other big difference is size. Seth is lean, a runner when he chooses to work out, but one who doesn't do any kind of strength-training, where Mitchell looks like he spends his time rolling those huge tractor tire things across the parking lot at his shop or bench-pressing hundreds of pounds in a gym.

Don't get me wrong, he's not *huge*, but his muscles are all clearly defined, and he has the body of a man who's ten years younger than he is. Mitchell also has probably four or five inches on Seth, who's only three inches taller than me. At least, that's what he says. I'd say it's more like one or two inches because we're almost eye-to-eye.

"Hailey," Seth says my name like it's the last word he ever wants to say, or maybe just like he's pissed I'm not here alone. That makes it harder for him to try to intimidate me, which is most of the reason Mitchell said he was coming. Maybe we should introduce my ex to his ex and let them make each other miserable.

Nah. I dismiss that thought quickly. They're too much alike, they won't ever get along.

"Hi, Seth." I greet him but turn my attention to my son. "Look, Connor. It's your daddy. Can you say hi?"

Connor ignores both of us, crouching down on the ground instead to run his toy trucks across the asphalt. Seth sighs, exasperated, and probably irritated by the fact that his son isn't paying any attention, but he's *three*. His attention span is about the same as a gnat's.

When a few minutes go by and Connor still doesn't acknowledge him, Seth turns his ire on me. "Really, Hailey? You're just going to let him play in the parking lot where anything can happen to him?"

He did not *just say that to me.*

Before I can tell him to kiss my ass, I'm staring at Mitchell's back because he's suddenly standing between

157

us. "Don't even start, asshole." His voice is a don't-fuck-with-me growl that has the space between my legs turning damp instantly. I *love* that he's standing up for me this way.

Letting Mitchell handle Seth would be great, but I know in the long run it will only make things more difficult because he won't always be here to be the mountain standing between us.

As much as I hate to do it, I step around Mitchell and turn to face him. "Let me handle this," I tell him in a low voice. He doesn't want to let me; I can tell by the way he clenches his jaw to keep from telling me *hell* no.

Once I'm sure he's going to stay quiet, I turn to my ex. "You act like I set him down in the middle of a busy parking lot and left him to go sit down and drink a margarita. Nothing could be further from the truth. He's right here," I point down to where Connor is sitting between us "I would *never* let something happen to my son."

I expect him to say something, to argue further with me, but he doesn't. After a quick look at Mitchell that has me clenching my hands at my side, because dammit, *I'm* the one he should be scared of right now, not Mitchell, he turns away.

While I could argue and try to force him to listen to me, it would cause more trouble than it's worth. Instead, I pick Connor up despite his protesting. He doesn't want to be carried, so he struggles the whole time I'm holding him and doesn't calm down until I set him down in the soft grass of the playground.

This is when Seth decides he's ready to actually act like

a parent, so he walks over to us and crouches in front of his son, careful not to let his stupid pants touch the grass. He starts talking to Connor who's still mad he's not on the asphalt. The longer Connor ignores him, the more irritated I watch him become.

It shouldn't amuse me, but it does. I have to bite down on my lip to keep from smiling because this is what having a three-year-old is like *all the time*. They might say the twos are terrible, but it doesn't just suddenly stop on the third birthday. In fact, based on some of the ornery kids in my class, it might just continue until adulthood.

Mitchell's warmth hits my chest and he takes my hand in his, leading me over to one of the picnic tables close by. "C'mon, let's give them a little time to get to know each other. We can sit over here so you're close to Connor, but don't have to listen to him being a fucking pussy."

His words make me laugh so hard I snort. Seth's head snaps up so he can glare at us, but he wisely doesn't make any comments, so I relax.

"It's been a long week," Mitchell starts, trying to keep me distracted. "I don't know about you, but I'm glad it's finally the weekend."

Maybe for him it's been long. "For me, it felt like the week flew by because I was dreading today."

"Yeah, I can see that." He's holding my hand in both of his and rubbing my palm like he's massaging it.

It feels *so* good. "Mmm," I let out a small groan. Mitchell's fingers are *magical*. The thought makes me remember just how magical they were last weekend and I squeeze my thighs together to relieve some of the pressure.

"Hey now," he smiles devilishly down at me. "None of that when I can't do anything about it."

"Sorry," I say with a shrug, not really sorry at all.

Mitchell smiles down at our hands as he shakes his head. "No, you're not."

"You're right." I nudge his knee with mine, wanting him to look at me again. Having his eyes on me, the way he looks at me like I'm the only thing he sees, it makes me feel amazing, like I'm the most important thing to him. I *crave* the way he wants me. I want him the same way.

Being around him is like being a teenager again. The butterflies in your stomach when you first meet a guy, the nervousness that comes with being around him, and having all his attention centered on you. It's a heady feeling, one I don't want to get rid of anytime soon.

We haven't been sitting here very long, maybe twenty minutes, when Seth calls my name. When I turn my attention back to him, he's standing, brushing off his pristine pants. As much as I want to stay where I am, I walk back towards him to see what he wants since he's just staring at me, waiting for something. I just don't know what until I'm standing before him.

Seth looks down at the expensive watch on his arm. "I need to get going, I have plans."

"You're kidding me, right?" I can't believe him. Well, that's not true. I *can*, I just hoped for better when I should've known to expect the least amount.

He ignores the anger coming out in my voice and runs his hands over his hair like he's afraid even one single hair has dared defy him. "No, Hailey. I'm not *kidding* you. I'll call you to set up a time to get Connor next time."

"Get him?" The hell? "What do you mean *get him*? I'm not letting you take him somewhere when he barely knows you. You're going to need to spend actual *time* with him for a while before you can just pick him up and take him without me."

Seth groans like I'm being unreasonable, but I'm not. *He's* being ridiculous. Our son is *three* and he hasn't seen him in over a year. Our divorce was final fifteen months ago, and it had been a while before then, so it's actually closer to two years.

"We can talk about this later."

I don't want to talk *later*, but since he walks away *as* he's speaking and Connor has now decided he wants to play on the equipment twenty feet away, I don't have the option to go after him. My son is more important.

Mitchell doesn't come with me, and it's not until after I've put Connor in the swing and started pushing that I see him at Seth's car. They're talking, surprisingly it looks like it's a civil conversation. I split my attention between the swing and what's going on with the two of them, watching as Mitchell's face becomes stormy and he leans forward menacingly.

Whatever he says to Seth has him hurrying to get inside his car and leave. I bet he locked the door the second it shut to keep Mitchell out, something that makes me laugh a little. How did I never notice how Seth avoided confrontation with anyone he wasn't sure he could best? I just can't get over how quickly he backed down from whatever he was saying.

Making his way over to us, I can tell Mitchell's still pissed about whatever they were talking about. When he reaches me, he doesn't say anything, just puts his arm around my waist and watching as I push Connor's swing.

I can't take the suspense, so after a couple of minutes, I ask, "What was that all about?"

"Nothing really," he says with a nonchalant shrug. "Just wanted to make a few things clear." Mitchell's head shakes, but he's smirking. "How the hell did you end up with an asshole like that?"

Now I'm the one shrugging. "Young and dumb, I guess? At least I finally figured it out."

He laughs. "Yeah, I don't know about that. I'm an asshole too."

"Maybe." I consider him, tilting my head to one side so I can act like I'm trying to come to a decision. When I don't dispute his statement, his hand at my waist digs in and I jump. I'm not super ticklish, but he found the spot that will have me writhing on the ground shrieking.

I try to get away, but the way he's holding me prevents me from moving far. Now that he knows it's a ticklish spot, he pulls me so I'm standing in front of him and he can get to it better. I start to giggle and try to squirm away, but he has his other arm wrapped around my chest. I'm stuck, and the harder I laugh the louder Connor's giggles get. He can't even see what Mitchell's doing to me, but my laughter is contagious.

Soon, we're all laughing, and when Mitchell stops torturing me, I relax into his embrace. The grin on my face is so wide my cheeks kinda hurt. *This* is the type of family I wanted to have when I found out I was pregnant. I pray it continues because losing this now would tear my heart into unrecognizable pieces.

CHAPTER 25

Mitchell

The next three weeks pass quickly, between work, the kids and their activities, and spending time with Hailey. Before I know it's close, Evie's recital weekend is upon us and I'm going to be forced into spending time with my ex. I want to watch Evie dance, but listening to Tabitha critique everything the kids do is not how I want to spend my Saturday. I'd much rather be with Hailey. Hailey, her son, and my kids would be even better.

I've been waiting for Tabitha to say something about me dating, sure the kids would tell her the first time they saw her after Hailey and Connor came to our place for dinner. Surprisingly, there's been nothing and she's been civil the past couple times I've had to see her. I keep waiting for the real Tab to show up, but so far, it's been nice.

The auditorium is already filling up when I walk in, and I see a lot of the guys I've become friendly with since Evie and Sophie are friends. Plus, they all bring their cars to my shop now. It's always a good idea to be friendly with your mechanic. We're the ones who keep your vehicle running smoothly, which means less money coming out of your pocket for little things.

There are a few seats free near them, so I go down and take one. Maybe the rest of the seats nearby will get filled and Tabitha will have to sit elsewhere. One can hope maybe.

When they see me, Isaac and Caleb both reach out hands to clasp mine in greeting since they're close, while the others raise hands or nod once to show they've seen me. The seats on either side of Isaac are open, so I take the one furthest away from their family, figuring the other is where Stacey is sitting. She's probably back right now helping Sophie get into her costume.

With the way Tabitha is, me going back to help Evie would make sense, but dance recitals are the one area where she turns into a perfectionist parent. She always wants Evie to look better than everyone else, probably because it makes her look good too.

I'm listening to Isaac and his brothers discuss Will's season this year, ribbing him about an interception he made in his last game when someone sits down beside me. Turning, I see Hailey's bright smile.

"Hi," she says softly. "Is Evie excited for today?"

I'm so surprised to see her I can't respond immediately. Finally, I snap out of it to tell her, "Yeah, she called me last night *and* this morning to make sure I was still coming." Shaking my head at the memory, I smile. "Like I'd ever miss one of her recitals."

Hailey lays her hand on top of mine where it rests on my thigh and squeezes. "She knows better than to think that. I'm sure the excitement and nerves were getting to her." Her lips lift in a small smile. "All little girls want their dads to be there when they're nervous. It helps, just knowing you're here."

I return hers with a smile of my own, then lean forward to greet the woman sitting beside her. "Hey, Riley. I didn't expect to see you today."

The brunette shrugs one shoulder. "The girls told us about today's recital a few weeks ago at brunch and we decided to come show our support. Plus, at least half these kids are my patients. It's nice to see them in a setting when they aren't mad because they're seeing me the same day they have to get shots." Her lips twist, but she laughs.

A few minutes later, parents start coming out of the back to take their seats, so I know it's almost time to start. The wives of some of the guys sitting here in our section stop to say hello to Hailey and Riley, and me too as they go past. Stacey leans down to hug both girls, then kisses me on the cheek as she squeezes by before Isaac pulls her down on his lap, smacking a loud kiss on her lips that makes her shriek and laugh.

Everyone around us laughs, but I pray they haven't gotten the attention of Tabitha. If she sees me, she's going to come over, and with Hailey and I holding hands I know she'll cause a scene.

I haven't seen her come out though, and it makes me worry she hasn't gotten here yet. Was her car in the lot when I got here? I can't remember. A soft hand lands on the one Hailey's not touching, and I look over at Stacey. "Tabitha's still back there with Evie. They were having trouble with the braid she was trying to put in her hair. It's just like the one Sophie has, which is why Evie wanted it. She wouldn't let me show her, or do it, and finally pulled up a video that got her started."

Stacey rolls her eyes, acting like it's not that big a deal, but I groan inwardly. Tabitha's always causing a problem. Why couldn't she just let someone help her? It's just a braid, not the cure for cancer.

We sit chatting for a few more minutes before the rest of the parents come out, but by then the lights have lowered and it's harder to see who's sitting where. Luckily for me, Tabitha doesn't come over here, so I relax as the owners of the studio come up on stage to greet everyone.

Meredith steps forward first. "Good afternoon everyone. We're so happy you're here, and I know all the dancers backstage are thankful for your support. They've all worked hard, and I know they're excited to show you what they've learned so far."

She's still speaking when Hailey leans closer to me to whisper, "Why are they having a recital so early in the year? Aren't recitals normally in the spring or early summer?"

"This one is more, I guess, a practice recital. Competition season starts after the first of the year and having a smaller one early gets out some of the kids' nerves so they can focus better. Mostly, I think they just like being able to dress up and have everyone clap for them. The little kids especially."

Hailey nods as Meredith finishes her speech and introduces Jax, who blows her a kiss when she takes a step back to let him have the spotlight. "Thanks, Sweet Tart," he says to her before turning his attention to all of us. "Welcome. We're glad to have you all here today. I just want to tell you all to make sure you cheer loudly, but only *after* each performance is finished. Don't randomly yell your child's name when they come on stage because it distracts and flusters them. That's when they make mistakes."

He looks toward the area where we're all sitting and using his fingers, gestures from his eyes to our group. "I'm looking at you, Montgomerys."

The rest entire auditorium laughs, and I lean over to explain to Hailey, "Some members," I point at Will and Meredith's husband Mark, "like to single out their family members when they come out onto the stage, and last year, Sophie tripped when they yelled. I'm fairly sure they're the reason Meredith and Jax do this early recital. To let them get out all their yelling *before* competition starts."

She giggles, and hearing what I'm saying, Isaac chuckles beside me too. Jax finishes up his speech, saying, "Enjoy! We'll see you at the end."

They walk off the stage and a few moments later the first group of kids come out. These ones are about Connor's age, and I hear Hailey's quiet, "Awww," when she sees them toddle out behind their teacher. "They're so cute!"

I turn my hand over and thread my fingers with hers, holding her hand like we're teenagers on our first date but loving every moment of it. We watch the smallest kids do their dance, even though they're basically just following whatever their teacher is doing. They have no clue if the moves they're making are the right ones, which just makes them more charming.

When they're finished, the whole auditorium claps for them, and the little kids just wave at us all. They all have huge smiles on their faces, and the applause doesn't stop until the last one leaves the stage. That means a *lot* of clapping because the last child goes in the opposite direction of everyone else and the teacher has to run after her. It makes everyone laugh, which is nice.

There are two more groups before Evie and Sophie come on. They try hard not to look out into the audience to find their parents, but I can tell they're struggling to stay strong. It's kind of adorable.

They start their routine and I'm a little in awe of Meredith and Jax. I don't know how they come up with the choreography for these dances, but they manage to make each one unique. Not one of the groups today does the same routine or even one that's similar. I don't think I could manage that. But then, I didn't choreograph dances for a megastar either the way they did. Not many people can do that. Their reputation is why Tabitha chose this school. I'm glad she did because Evie loves dance and this is the best school in Seattle, maybe the state.

Once they finish their routine, the Montgomery crew all yells for Sophie, and they cheer along with me for Evie too. Hailey cheers for everyone, not wanting to single one out, I'm sure, since she teaches more than just Sophie and Evie. She and Riley both do this.

The girls file off the stage and we watch the rest of the groups do their dances. Hailey's entranced by them all if her soft gasps and sighs are anything to go by, but I'm impatient for it to be over now that Evie's danced. I want to grab her and hug her, tell her what a good job she did and how proud I am of her.

By the time the last dance finishes, I'm almost unable to sit still. The thigh our hands is resting on is bouncing up and down and I'm struggling to remain in my seat. The second Meredith and Jax finish thanking us for coming and saying how proud they are of all the dancers them-selves, I'm out of my seat, dragging Hailey behind me.

Normally, I would go backstage and see Evie, but since Hailey is with me, I stay up front, holding the flowers I brought for her in my free hand. I'm glad setting them on the floor at the edge of the floor where it met the next set of seats didn't ruin them. I was afraid if I held them the whole time, I'd crush them while I waited to be able to give them to her.

A person comes to stand beside me, but I pay them no attention, thinking it's just another parent, but then she speaks, and I realize Tabitha's been so far from my thoughts I forgot she was even here.

"Did you just get here?" She asks it like it's just a normal question, but I can *feel* the anger behind it.

I make it a point not to look at her when I answer, not wanting to see the ire I'm sure is reflected in her expres-sion. "No, I got here ten minutes or so before it started. I sat with the Montgomery's."

"Oh," she says snottily, put out because it's one less reason to complain. "Who's that?" I don't know if she hasn't looked close enough to recognize her, or if she's forgotten what Hailey looks like, but I'm thankful either way. The last thing Evie needs is us to fight here in the company of all her classmates.

Hailey stiffens beside me, and I know she's waiting for the fireworks to start too. "My girlfriend," I finally respond, praying my luck holds and it's that she doesn't realize who she is.

Tabitha sniffs, and I know she's lifting her nose higher in the air, thinking she's much more important than she is. "Girlfriend? I didn't realize you had any of those. I thought you were more the one-night stand type." She's trying to rile Hailey up, but she knows I haven't slept with anyone since the day I met her, so it doesn't work.

Leaning around me, Tabitha holds out her hand to Hailey like she's expecting her to take it and kiss the top. I roll my eyes at her ridiculousness but bite the inside of my cheek to keep from calling her on it. "Hello, girlfriend. I'm the wife."

Motherfucker.

"Ex. Wife." I bite out from between clenched teeth. Turning to glare at her, I wish I could smack the smug as fuck look off her face. She thinks she's causing a problem, but if she realized who Hailey is, she'd know that's impossible.

Before she can try to stir the pot any further, Evie comes running out from behind the curtain. "Daddy!" she screeches, throwing herself in my arms and wrapping her arms tight around my neck.

I stand, bringing her up with me. Evie wraps her legs around my waist as I spin her around. "I'm so proud of you, princess. You did such a great job."

"Thanks, Daddy," she says, her words muffled because her face is buried in my neck.

After twirling her around a few times, I put her down and turn her to face her mom. Tabitha hugs her too, murmuring something in her ear I can't hear before she stands to her full height. "C'mon, Evie. We need to get going. I still have to pick Ben up at Charlie's."

"But, Mommy…" Evie whines, face falling because she doesn't want to leave just yet.

We're saved when Stacey steps over, her hand on Sophie's shoulder. "Hey, Tab. Sophie wants to know if Evie can come home with us for a sleepover. They're both so excited about today. I don't think they're ready for it to end yet."

At first, she looks like she's going to say no. Evie and Sophie are both holding their hands up under their chins like they are praying and saying, "Please, please, *please*," until finally Tabitha relents with a beleaguered sigh.

"Great," Stacey says with a big smile. "I'll call you tomorrow to figure out a time to bring her back."

Tabitha's attention is already on her phone, so she just nods before turning to walk away. She doesn't even say goodbye to Evie, not that Evie notices. She and Sophie are still jumping up and down with glee over their sleepover.

"Thank you." The two words aren't enough to adequately convey my gratitude, but Stacey gets it.

"No problem. I'm just glad she gets to stay and celebrate." She turns back to look at their family, then turns back to Hailey and I. "We're all going to Isaac's parents for a barbecue they're throwing to celebrate the success of the recital… and also because none of us want to cook after this and no restaurant will have enough room *and* privacy so we can eat without gawkers. We'd love for you to join us."

I look down at Hailey. "What do you think?"

She smiles. "Why not? It will give you a little time with Evie too."

Her voice reveals her presence to Evie and Sophie, and they both run over to hug her when they see her. Small voices talk over each other as they both try to get her attention, so she crouches down to be on their level and gets them to take turns telling her all about the recital and ask what she thought. Hailey's in her element with the kids, and the longer they talk, the more kids come over to join.

Not all of them are in Hailey's class, but it's clear she makes it a point to talk to every child she encounters at the school because she knows a lot of them by name. Watching her with these kids makes me fall a little harder for her. She's everything I could ever want in a mother for my kids. Granted, they already have one, but they would definitely benefit from having Hailey and her warmth in their lives on a more full-time basis.

The thoughts going through my head have me off-balance. I swore when my relationship with Tabitha turned to shit that I would *never* do the marriage thing again, but here I am thinking about Hailey in that context. It's crazy how much she's come to mean to me in such a short time. I just hope she feels the same.

CHAPTER 26

Hailey

*A*fter a quick phone call to my mom to make sure she's okay with keeping Connor longer that ends with her agreeing to keep him until tomorrow, I ride with Mitchell over to the Montgomery's. I could ride with Riley since she's invited too, but I want to be with him.

We're the last ones to get to the house, and when we walk through to the backyard it's full of people standing together in groups. Some are holding the smallest children, while there are others holding margarita glasses or bottles of beer.

Isaac is the first to see us. He comes over to greet us and thank us for coming, then leads us over to two older couples standing close to the grill.

"Dad, this is Sophie's teacher, Hailey. Hailey, my dad, Steven."

173

The man turns away from where he's flipping burger patties on the grill to hold out his hand for me to shake. "Ah. I've heard a lot about you. Sophie loves having you as a teacher. She's especially fond of the reading nook you have set up in your classroom."

Beaming at him, I lean forward to confide, "It's my favorite spot too. And, I love having her in my class. Sophie's such a sweet girl."

He grins back at me, then turns to greet Mitchell. It's obvious they've met before, but since Sophie and Evie are good friends, that's not surprising at all. Isaac introduces me to his mom next, and her response is much the same as his dad's. "Hi, Hailey. I'm glad you," she lifts her head to smile at Mitchell too, "and Mitch could make it. Sophie has told us so much about you and your class."

Mitchell joins us before I can say anything, placing his hand possessively on the small of my back and leaning forward to kiss her cheek. "Hey Gail, thanks for having us."

He's making it clear that we're here together, but I can't help but wonder if he was ever here with his ex-wife. I'm sure he was and start to worry about what everyone here is thinking. The parents especially. Are they wondering why he's here with me and not her? Do they all know the relationship ended?

What am I thinking? Mitchell and Tabitha split more than a year ago. Surely, they knew before today. They'd have to. I need to stop obsessing.

"Hailey?" Mitchell's voice brings me out of my head, and I look up to see him staring down at me, brows furrowed as he studies my face. "Everything okay?"

174

My face heats, but I manage to nod. "Yeah, sorry. Long day." I try to shrug it off, but I don't think he believes me. Since we're around all these other people, he lets it go, at least for now.

The introductions continue, and next, I'm introduced to parents of one of the girl's husbands. I'm not sure which because all the names kind of run together for me, but all too soon Mitchell and I are split up. He goes over to hang out with Isaac and the rest of the men while I head over to where the women are all sitting and chatting.

As I take a seat beside Riley, she hands over a glass of what looks to be a frozen margarita. I take a long drink of the icy concoction, hoping the injection of alcohol will help me relax. I know a few of these women from brunch, but they aren't all familiar.

The conversation between them all flows, and I'm happy to sit here and just listen. My glass is quickly empty, and when I sit back from refilling it, a man is standing behind the woman sitting directly across from me, grabbing the baby out of her arms.

Holy...

I'm speechless. In fact, I don't think my brain will ever work again. I made a fool out of myself when I met Will, but this guy is on a whole different level.

They both notice me staring dumbly, and the woman starts to snicker, covering her mouth with a hand now that her arms are free. "I think you have a fan, Luke."

"Hey there," he says, one side of his mouth tipping up into a smile, but it looks forced.

I bet he's always fending off fan attention... and prob-ably wasn't expecting to have to do it here. As hard as it is,

I attempt to stop my fangirling and act like a normal human. "Uh, hi." My voice comes out all breathy, and I want to crawl under the chair I'm sitting on and hide. He probably thinks I'm an idiot.

Riley leans over, putting her arm around my shoulders and trying not to laugh at my giant faux pas. "I guess you forgot that conversation we had at brunch, huh?"

Turning to her, I try to glare, but my eyes are pretty much bugging out of my head still. "Ya think?"

"Sorry?" She doesn't look like it *at all*. None of them look sorry at my reaction.

Jules, one of the girls I met at brunch, pats him on the hand. "It's okay, Luke. We won't let her take your picture."

This is clearly an inside joke because she and Natalie burst into giggles, their heads tilting together as they try to hold each other upright. Luke huffs out a breath, rolling his eyes skyward and saying, "Why me?" No one answers, and he leaves, taking the bundle in his arms with him.

Once Jules and her friend calm down, they look over at me. "I'm sorry, we really should have warned you he was here, but we don't think about it much anymore. It's hard to think of him as *Movie Star Luke* when he's been *Covered in vomit Luke* more than once at this point."

"Oddly enough," I tell her, "that visual helps a lot for me too." I'm still a little awestruck because I mean, he's *Luke Williams*! My inner teenager squeals in delight, but I shut her down quickly. "Are there any other famous people I should know about before I make a fool of myself again?"

Jules taps a finger against her lips, thinking. "No, don't

think so. Not anyone who's here at any rate. You already know Meredith used to work with Starla, and Will, well, no one cares about him besides Meg. I think you're good."

That's a relief. I quickly suck back my fresh margarita, needing the liquid courage to get through the rest of this party. As much as I want to, I don't gulp down the next one, because if I do, I'm going to be *drunk* and that won't end well for me. I'll probably wind up telling Luke's wife all about my crush on her husband and how I had so many pictures of him on my wall when I was younger. *That* would be too embarrassing to come back from, I think.

I'm saved from the danger of making a bigger fool of myself because Gail calls us over for dinner. Mitchell's waiting at the edge of the yard for me to meet him, and when I do, he looks down at the glass in my hand then into my eyes. "How many of those have you had?"

"A couple?" I don't want to admit to him that this is my third.

He moves in so he can speak directly into my ear. "Don't drink anymore, okay?" I start to lean back to ask why, but he continues, his words making my legs tremble along with other, more *private* parts of my body. "I have plans for you later since we're both kidless for the night."

Oh boy. "Can we leave now?" I ask, my lips brushing his ear.

His hand grips my hip hard enough to leave marks. "I wish," he mutters before tugging my lobe with his teeth. "C'mon, let's go eat. The sooner we eat, the sooner we can get out of here."

We take our seats at the table and I can't even tell you

what I eat. My thoughts are so focused on what Mitchell's *plans* are for tonight I'm unable to concentrate on anything else. I'm sure I respond to words that are said to me, but I couldn't tell you who said it or what was said.

It feels like it's hours later when Mitchell finally pushes his chair back from the table. "Thanks for inviting us, but we need to get going."

Riley and Meg, the two women sitting across from me both give me knowing looks and I can feel my blush reaching all the way to the roots of my hair. Trying to play it off, I smile at them both and give a little shrug.

"Talk to you later?" Riley lifts an eyebrow when she asks the question, then she looks between Mitchell and I like she's trying to make sure I'm sober enough to make this decision. The food helped soak up a lot of the alcohol in my system, so now I'm just excited and nervous for whatever is going to happen when we get back to the apartments.

"I'll text you in the morning," I assure her.

She still doesn't look totally convinced, but she nods. "You better."

We say goodbye to the rest of the group and the ride back seems to take half as long as it should. Mitchell pulls into a parking spot, then turns to face me.

"I want you." The words are matter of fact. Maybe even blunt. There's no way to take them other than how he means.

It's hard for me to say them, but I manage, my voice breaking when I say, "I want you too." I do. I want to be with him in every way I can be. My only concern is that my body doesn't look the way it did when I first met Seth.

I've carried a baby, given birth, and my stomach isn't completely flat anymore. I have stretch marks and a little pooch.

Mitchell helps me out of his truck, and I wonder which apartment we're going to. Will it be mine? Or his? I could save myself the question and just ask, but he starts practically dragging me across the parking lot, so the answer is pretty obvious.

His apartment is much quieter than it was the last time I was here. It's cleaner too. You can tell the kids haven't been here because there aren't any sneakers or schoolbooks laying around.

I don't get to admire the living room very long because he continues walking quickly until we're in his room. The moment the door shuts, he's on me, crowding me back against it until I can't move.

Mitchell's arms land on either side of my head and I'm trapped in every way. All I can smell is his cologne mixed with the faint scent of oil and car parts that never seems to go away completely. His body surrounds me, and the margaritas I drank earlier have nothing on how he makes me feel.

His mouth drops to mine and our night really begins.

CHAPTER 27

Mitchell

A small whimper leaves her mouth when my tongue demands entrance. Hailey tastes so *damn* good. I want to kiss her forever, explore every nook and cranny of her mouth with my tongue, but I also want inside her more than I want my next breath.

Her hands come up to grip my waist, clutching my shirt and pulling it taut. My body is pressed against her, so close I can feel the tight buds of her nipples against my chest and the way her legs shift restlessly. She wants me as much as I want her. The knowledge makes me feel like a fucking *king*.

As much as I don't want to release her lips, I need her to be naked... *now*. Leaning back, I reach down and grip the hem of her shirt in my hands, doing my best not to just rip it off her body in my haste to finally see her.

"Lift your hands." The command leaves my lips and she hurries to obey, releasing my shirt to put her arms up over her head. The shirt clears her head and I suck in a breath. The sight of her tits has me almost coming in my jeans, and that's before her bra comes off.

Her chest is heaving, breaths coming fast, and almost a pant. She looks like a goddamn goddess and she's all fucking *mine*. It's hard to bring my eyes up from her chest, but I want to make sure she's still with me.

Hailey's eyes are glazed with passion, but when I meet her gaze, she nods, knowing what I'm looking for. Her tongue comes out to swipe along her lower lip and I accept the invitation. She brings her arms down to wrap them around my neck and presses close, bringing her back away from the door which is perfect for what I want to do next.

Her tongue sweeps my mouth as I unhook her bra, letting it fall to the floor between us. Another of those noises fills my mouth, and as much as I love having her here at my mercy, I'm dying to see her spread out on my bed. I want to see what her hair looks like fanning across my pillow and what her pale body looks like against my dark sheets.

My mouth doesn't leave hers as I maneuver us across the room, using my body to follow hers down onto the bed before I finally release her. She looks up at me, dazed, then lifts up on her elbows, realizing where we are now.

"You're pretty good at that." She grins, and I have to laugh. I love that she's teasing me, even when the moment is as heavy as this one is.

As much as I don't want to get up, I move so she can

push herself up the bed until her head is on the pillows, I wanted them to be on only a few seconds ago. The sight is as amazing as I thought it would be.

"Take off your pants." Hailey moves quickly, unsnapping the button before lowering her zipper, but it's not fast enough. I'm faster, pulling off her shoes and then taking her pants by the hem and yanking them off too, leaving her in nothing but a pair of lavender panties.

I run one hand down my face before looking back at her. The sight of her almost naked in my bed is the best thing I've seen in a long-ass time.

"Your turn." Her voice is sultry, begging me to do dirty things to her.

My eyes stay on hers as I pull off my shirt, loving the way she bites down on her lip when she sees my bare chest. I work hard at the gym to keep in shape and I can tell she appreciates it. My hands lower to my jeans next, unbuttoning my fly slowly while she watches.

Hailey gasps when I shove them down my hips along with my underwear and I watch her eyes widen when my cock bobs free. I take myself in hand and stroke while she watches. Every movement of my hand has her eyes switching between my shaft and the way the muscles on my arm move.

I'm turned on, even more when she trails her hand between her breasts, down her stomach and under the band of her panties. Her hips jolt when her fingertips touch her clit and I wish the silk wasn't blocking me from being able to see exactly what she's doing.

The fabric moves with her hand and she starts to make those whimpering noises almost nonstop. I can only take a few minutes of watching before I pounce, crawling up between her spread legs from the bottom of the mattress and pressing my mouth against the inside of her thighs.

They quiver against my lips, the movement of her hand stopping as she watches me, waiting to see where I'm going to touch next. As much as I want to go right for her pussy, her tits are bouncing with the movement of her body and I want to give them all the attention I wasn't able to last time.

I put a hand on either side of her waist and dip down to take her left nipple between my lips. The hand not in her panties lands on the back of my head, her fingers tangling in my hair and I look up, brushing the hard knot with my beard.

"Please," she begs, trying to force my mouth back down against her flesh.

I don't think she even knows what she's asking for, but she's begging so prettily I can't resist. My eyes stay on hers as I run my tongue around her nipple before biting down on it lightly.

Her hips raise off the bid and a strangled moan comes out of her mouth, but I can tell she likes the hint of roughness in my touch. Using my fingers, I pluck her other nipple with my fingers while sucking the left one back into my mouth. The dual sensations have her tossing her head back and forth on the pillow, her eyes squeezed shut. I switch my mouth to the other, switching so I'm plumping the breast I just had in my mouth with my hand. I wouldn't want her to feel neglected after all.

Hailey's hand is yanking my hair, her other hand fisting and loosening at her side. Her thighs squeeze together like she's trying to relieve the pressure, but if anyone is going to do that, it's going to be me.

Letting her nipple leave my mouth with a pop, I move down so I'm kneeling beside her legs and slowly pull her panties down her thighs and over her ankles before dropping them carelessly off the side of the bed. I can't take my eyes off what I've just revealed.

She's completely bare, her pink flesh glistening with her arousal. I want to dive in and devour her, but I don't want to go too fast. I spread her legs, making room for me between them, and run my hands up her taut thighs. Her muscles are tense, quivering with anticipation, so I gently spread her lips with my thumbs, baring her pussy to my hungry gaze.

When I glance up, she's looking down at herself, her lip back between her teeth like she's trying to keep from making a sound.

"Can I?" I ask her permission, not because I think she may not want this, but because I want it to be her decision. I want her to know without a doubt that *she* asked for this.

Hailey looks confused at first, but quickly catches on. "Yes. Please, *God*, yes."

The second she gives me permission, I lean forward and lick from the bottom of her pussy to her clit. Her moan is loud, and I love that she doesn't even try to hide how much she likes what I'm doing.

My eyes stay on hers as I trace a circle around the hard rise of her clit, careful not to touch it directly, not yet. Then, I lick her again, this time starting at her clit and ending with my tongue inside her pussy.

She tastes better than I imagined, and trust me, I've imagined it a *lot*. I can't even count the number of times I jerked off thinking about her pussy after that night in her apartment. I've wanted nothing more than to be right here, well, right here *and* inside her.

I use my tongue the same way I soon will my cock, thrusting it in and out twice more before concentrating my attention back on her clit. This time I lick directly over it, then seal my mouth around it and suck in small pulses. Her legs tighten around my head and I know she likes what I'm doing to her.

Using two fingers, I slide them inside her, pushing deep enough to find the ridged spot I know will drive her crazy, making a come here motion until her clit starts to throb against my tongue. My suction deepens and when I take the first hard pull, she shatters, her body squeezing my fingers rhythmically.

Feeling that, I can't wait any longer to be inside her. I rise above her and reach over to grab a condom out of my nightstand, rolling down my length carefully while she watches, eyes heavy-lidded after her orgasm.

Hailey's body is relaxed now, her thoughts only on how good she feels which lets me get into position and stroke the head of my cock against her clit. She flinches, still sensitive, but now that I've got her attention, I notch the head of my dick at her entrance and slide in, slow and steady.

"*Fuck*, you're so damn tight." She fits me like a glove, like she was made to cradle my body in hers. I want to kiss her, so I lean over, planting my fists on either side of her head and touching my mouth to hers as I withdraw, my tongue entering her mouth at the same time I push back inside her pussy.

Her hands come up to clutch my biceps, nails digging in slightly and giving me the smallest hint of pain with the sting. Our hips move together, hers rising when I pull out like she wants to keep me deep inside.

I can feel her tightening around me, but I want her to come again. I'm not going to be able to hold out much longer, she feels too damn good, and I want to watch one more time before I go over the edge.

With that goal in mind, I straighten so I'm kneeling between her legs, hating to lose her mouth but wanting to make this good for her. I press down on her clit with my thumb, drawing small circles on the hard knot, my eyes never leaving hers.

Her neck arches, eyes sliding closed as her moans get louder and I start to move faster. She's getting closer, I can tell, so I use my free hand to grab her thigh, spreading her wide so I can thrust deeper. The change in angle is what she needs, and I can feel myself rubbing against the spot inside that's guaranteed to drive her wild.

I know she's about to come when her back bows, her body stiffens, and she lets out a keening cry. Her pussy squeezes me so tight I can barely move, but that's fine. If I try to move, I'm just going to come, so I stay where I am until her body relaxes and her grip on me loosens.

I'm beyond ready for my own release, so I pick up my pace, pounding inside her until I explode, wishing I were coming inside *her* instead of a fucking condom.

What the hell?

What kind of thought is that? I can't concentrate on it

too much because it feels like my brain has completely left my body. Letting myself enjoy being inside her for a few minutes, I press a quick kiss to her lips, loving the blissed-out look on her face.

Finally, I have to get out of bed and deal with the condom, and when I come back, Hailey's passed out in my bed. I slide in beside her, wrapping my arm around her waist and pulling her back to my front. As much as I want to know where her head is at, I'm glad she's comfortable enough with me to be able to sleep.

My own eyes slowly shut, and I allow myself to follow her into sleep. Tomorrow is soon enough to talk about what this means, what I want from her.

CHAPTER 28

Hailey

*P*arent-teacher conferences are quickly becoming my least favorite thing. Every parent is convinced their child is the smartest one ever, and I get it, truly I do. The problem? Not every child does well on standardized tests, not all of them turn in their work on time—or at all—and some of them aren't the easiest to get along with either.

Don't get me wrong. Some of the conferences *have* been pleasant. Those parents are awesome, their kids are even better, and they make being a teacher look easy. Unfortunately, for every good conference, it seems like I have two horrible ones.

Like the last one. Tommy Ramsey is a holy terror in class and probably out of it. He talks back, refuses to do work, and is just generally disruptive during class. After meeting his dad, I know where he gets it from. The man spends more time staring at my chest than actually listening to what I'm trying to tell him.

He makes me feel downright dirty. I wish I had a second sweater I could put on because even though my shirt covers every part of my cleavage, he's making me feel like I'm wearing a bikini top. I feel bad for his wife. She's timid and flinches every time I say something about her son. She knows how he is; she just can't get help from her husband in dealing with him.

Tommy Senior's response to his son's behavior is, "Boys will be boys, am I right?"

"No, Mr. Ramsey, you're not right." I hear his wife suck in a breath, though I'm not sure if it's because I just disagreed with her husband or because she thinks his reaction is going to be bad.

The man puffs out his chest. It's not a good look for him because it just makes his portly stomach look bigger. "Now, you listen here," he starts, but I'm not about to let him talk like this to me.

"Mr. Ramsey. Your son interrupts my teaching at least once a day. I've tried to speak to you and your wife multiple times about this, but you always tell me you're busy. The only reason you're here today is because it's mandatory and we both know it. You need to speak to him. I'll be happy to help you figure out what's going on with him, but if it continues, there will be disciplinary action."

I look up at the clock and my heart speeds up. It's time

for this conference to end and my next to start. I'm both anticipating and dreading it because it's Evie's conference, which means I get to see Mitchell, but it also means I'll have to see her mom. That part I am *not* looking forward to.

"Now, if you'll come with me, it's time for my next conference. If you need more of my time, we can set up a second meeting." He grumbles all the way to the door, and when I open it, I see Mitchell standing just outside.

Evie isn't with him, which is probably for the best. She's doing great anyway, so the meeting part of this should be short. I'm sort of hoping I'll have a chance to just let him hold me, especially after that last meeting. *God*, I hate parents who don't give a shit.

Mr. Ramsey says something as he passes Mitchell that has him start to move towards him, a scary look on his face. "Mr. Anderson, if you'll come this way?" I say it more to keep him from beating the crap out of another parent in the hallway than anything else, but it works.

He raises an eyebrow at me, and I know it's because of the "Mr. Anderson" comment. I turn away, not wanting my heated face easily seen by the other two people in the hallway, and walk into my class, praying he's going to follow.

Once it's just the two of us, he shuts the door and comes over to wrap his arms around me. "Bad meeting?"

"*Ugh.* The worst. I swear that man doesn't care what his son does. It's probably the reason *why* his son does whatever he wants. Tommy's desperate for someone's attention and has decided even bad attention is good."

Mitchell shakes his head. "Not good." No, it's really not. I'm saved from replying when his lips land on mine. All thoughts of Mr. and Mrs. Ramsey, along with every other crappy meeting I had today leave my head when he touches me. And when he kisses me? Well, I'm lucky I remember my own name.

The kiss is entirely too short. It would probably be longer, but I hear the echo of heels in the hallway and figure it must be his ex-wife. I don't have long, but do manage to straighten my shirt and run my hands through my hair in an attempt to tame it from where his hands were all up in it a minute ago. There's nothing I can do about my swollen lips, but maybe she won't notice.

Tabitha Anderson walks in as I'm rounding my desk to take a seat. Mitchell drops into the one directly across from me, spreading his legs out and making himself comfortable. The contrast between him and Tabitha is so easy to see. She sits primly on the edge of the chair, her attention on whatever she's typing into her phone.

"Jesus, Tab, could you stop texting for five minutes so the teacher can tell us how our daughter is doing this year?" This meeting is *not* starting well. Mitchell's already irritated, whether because he had to stop touching me or because his ex isn't paying any attention to the meeting we're supposed to be having right now I'm not sure. It's probably both.

She waves away his question. "Oh, would you relax? It will only take me a minute to finish this."

Uh-oh. That's the *wrong* thing to say to him.

"Sure, of course. It's just, you know, our *daughter* we're

here to talk about. By all means," he flings one arm out towards the classroom, "finish your conversation first."

We sit in silence until she's finally ready to begin and I'm glad it didn't take her any longer because Mitchell is about to lose it. Tabitha finally puts her phone away, so I take advantage and start before he can lay into her the way I can tell he wants to.

"Evie is an absolute joy to have in my class. She's bright, inquisitive, and eager to learn everything she can. I wish all of my students were like her." Mitchell smiles, his pride in his daughter so easy to see. Tabitha isn't even looking at me. She's looking around the room, her focus on anything *but* me and I wonder why.

It's not like her to shy away from confrontation. At least, it wasn't last year when I first met her. I guess she might have changed since then, but it seems doubtful. Nothing else about her has changed.

Pulling out her folder, I lay it out in the middle of the desk and go over all the different metrics and where Evie is hitting on each one. "If you look here," I point to one, "she's doing especially well in Reading. She's reading on a sixth-grade level which is higher than the majority of the kids in class. I've been bringing in books from the school library to satisfy her thirst for books, but before I recommend any on the fifth and sixth-grade list, I wanted to get your thoughts. Some of those books are a bit more mature, and I don't know how you'd feel about her reading them." I lift two more sheets of paper, setting one down in front of each of them so they have it. "Here's the list for those grades. Please look over it and let me know what you think."

We go over the rest of her progress and thankfully, the meeting is over with almost ten minutes to spare. Neither parent asks any questions, and as soon as I say she can, Tabitha hightails it out of my room with her face buried in her phone screen.

Mitchell comes around my desk, resting his behind on the edge of my desk and taking both my hands in his, pulling me up so I'm standing between his legs. Once I'm where he wants me, he drops my hands and wraps his arms around my waist to pull me even closer.

My palms rest on his pecs and I lean in to kiss him. This kiss is soft, more tender than most of our kisses. I love the feeling of his tongue stroking the side of mine. I'm not sure how long we stand here, but neither of us hears the door open.

"*What the hell is this?*" Tabitha shrieks so loud I'm a little surprised the windows don't shatter.

Mitchell and I spring apart like two teenagers caught in my bedroom by my father. Maybe that's a bit too specific, but it's true. I turn my head to look at her and she's standing just inside the open door, hands on her hips and no lie, her hair is flying out behind her. She looks like the villain in a superhero movie. The one who *wants* to be a superhero and tries so hard to fit in.

I may be losing it a bit. Maybe it's lack of oxygen because I don't think I've taken a breath since she walked back in.

"Tabitha," Mitchell starts, taking a step like he's going to walk over to her.

She holds up a hand to stop him. "Oh no, you don't. What the hell are you and Evie's *teacher* doing? Isn't that against the rules? You're not supposed to *fuck* your child's teacher, Mitchell. Surely you know this."

Please tell me she did not just insinuate that Mitchell is only sleeping with me because I'm Evie's teacher. That is so not the case.

"Tabitha." Mitchell tries again, but she ignores him.

Taking a step back, she shakes her head. "I'm going right to the principal. He should know what type of teacher he hired." Her eyes narrow on me, and I literally *feel* the blood drain from my face when I see her remember who I am. Turning her attention to Mitchell now, she sneers, eyes full of disgust.

"You have *got* to be kidding me. How long has this been going on?" She gestures between us. "I thought you said *nothing happened* that day at the garage. You *promised* me nothing happened Mitchell. You lying piece of shit."

Mitchell stiffens. "I didn't lie to you, Tabitha. Nothing did happen between us that day. Up until this school year, I haven't seen Hailey since she left the shop that day. You know damn well I never cheated on you. Can you say the same?"

Tabitha doesn't have a response to that. Her non-response is an answer itself and I watch as Mitchell nods. "Yeah, that's what I thought." His voice is bitter, but that's to be expected.

She turns, leaving my classroom, her head held high. Is she really going to try to get me fired for being in a relationship with her husband? Is it going to be a problem that we're dating? I can separate the Evie at home from the Evie at school. I want to chase after her, beg her not to say anything to the principal, but I don't get the chance.

Mitchell takes off after her, leaving me standing alone in the center of my classroom wondering what he's doing. I want to go after them both now, but I can't. My last conference of the day will be here any minute. I just hope I have a job after it's finished.

CHAPTER 29

Mitchell

abitha is stalking up the hallway when I leave Hailey's classroom. "Tabitha," I hiss, trying not to draw any more attention to us. She ignores me, but I know she had to hear me say her name. The acoustics in this hallway are amazing.

I continue following her until she's almost to the principal's office. Letting her sabotage Hailey's career isn't something I can do, so I speed up enough to grab her at the elbow and pull her onto a different hall.

"What are you doing?"

She looks up at me, faking confusion. "What do you mean? I told you back there. I'm going to go see what the principal has to say about this." Tabitha shakes her head and I hate when she does this. She's playing the part of the poor wife, the one who's husband abuses her in every way.

It couldn't be further from the truth, but if she goes to the principal, there's a very real possibility she'll cost Hailey her job. If that happens, I'll probably lose Hailey. I can't let that happen.

"Why? Why do you have to be this way? Hailey hasn't done anything to you, but you're going to try to ruin her career? And for what? You just want to be able to say you got one up on her for stealing your husband when you know that's not what happened."

Tabitha tries to say something, but I talk over her. "I never cheated on you, Tabitha, not even when I felt like I was going to be stuck in a marriage that made me miserable until Evie turned eighteen." I'm trying to explain it to her rationally, but the more I talk, the higher my voice rises. If I'm not careful, someone will hear us arguing and come to investigate. Then I won't have to worry about *Tabitha* being the reason the principal finds out about our relationship.

"After last summer, I didn't think I'd ever see Hailey again. She was so upset with me when she found out I was married, even though nothing happened between us. Her ex cheated on her, multiple times, so she would never willingly do that to someone else. Don't punish her for what you assume are my indiscretions. Don't punish *her* because you're still pissed off at me."

At this point, as much as I hate the thought of even doing it, I'm not above begging her. Tabitha looks away from me, indecision on her face. Her brows are pulled in and she starts nibbling on her thumbnail in a way I used to think was cute.

"Please, Tab."

She's still looking down at the opposite end of the hallway when she speaks. "You weren't supposed to leave me."

My head rears back. "Excuse me?"

"You weren't supposed to leave me." Her voice is stronger the second time she says it and she turns to glare at me.

Well, this isn't where I saw this conversation going. Her words throw me for a loop, and I can't think of anything to say at first. "Tabitha, why would you want me to say?" Surprisingly, I want to know the answer to this question. "We were both *miserable* and wishing we were anywhere else. Why on earth would you want to sentence us both to that?" Better yet why is this a conversation we haven't had in the past year? She brings this up *now*?

Tabitha doesn't immediately answer, and I grow impatient waiting for her to say something... *anything*.

"I know you weren't happy. I wasn't either, but I still loved you. I didn't want our relationship to just end either. I didn't want to have to explain to my father that I couldn't keep our relationship together."

That makes a little more sense. "Hell, if that was the only reason why, I would've talked to him for you." I'm trying to inject a little humor into our conversation because this is heavy shit. Plus, her dad always hated me. He probably would have been just fine with her leaving me, especially if she took the kids away from me when she did.

She finally cracks a genuine smile. "Yeah, well, I didn't think about that at the time." Tabitha exhales a breath, her shoulders sagging further. "Fine. I won't say anything to the principal about you two. I don't even know if she'd have a problem with it. I just wanted to hurt you... and her too."

I don't expect her to say she's sorry, and it's a good thing because she doesn't. Tabitha leaves me standing in the hallway, looking at her with my mouth dropped open because she sounded genuine. It's been a long time since she's been anything but a bitch to me. I don't know if I can trust it, but as soon as the front door shuts behind her, I hightail it back to Hailey's room.

She's not here. Where is she? She couldn't have just left, could she?

I spin around and go in the opposite direction, heading for the parking lot where she parks every morning. Hailey's car is gone, so she must've left while Tabitha and I were having our stupid heart to heart.

Now I run in the opposite direction, crashing out of the front doors and making a beeline for my truck. I have to get to her, to make her understand that my ex is, in fact, human and isn't going to ruin her life.

My truck skids into the apartment parking lot and I take up two spaces when I park. I'm in way too much of a hurry to worry about parking etiquette. If someone gets upset, they can kiss my fucking ass. I need to get to Hailey.

I take the stairs to her apartment two at a time, and by the time I reach her landing I'm breathing heavy and a little lightheaded. I guess I need to incorporate more running into my gym routine, but I could give a shit about that right now.

My fist pounds on her door as I scream her name. "Hailey!" The door doesn't budge. "Please let me in." Still nothing. I rest my head on her door frame and wish for her to open it.

"She's not in there."

I spin around and see Riley standing in her doorway, her eyes darting between me and Hailey's door. "Are you sure?"

"Yeah," she says. "She hasn't gotten home from school yet, but she should be here soon. I think she had conferences today. A few might have run late. Do you want to come in and wait for her?"

Instead of responding, I head for the stairs. Where could she be? I try her cell phone again as I'm jogging down to the first floor, but there's no answer.

As much as I don't want to admit defeat, I don't think I have a choice. Until she decides to talk to me, I'm screwed. I just hope she doesn't ignore me forever.

I'm walking up the stairs to my apartment, and when my floor comes into view, I see her standing at my apartment, her back resting on the wall beside my door and her arms crossed over her chest.

"*Hailey.*" The way I say her name, like it's both a curse and a prayer, grabs her attention and she looks up. I've barely cleared the top step when she comes barreling over to me and throws herself into my arms. Her arms wrap around my neck and her arms around my waist.

"Where have you been?"

Her head lifts from where she shoved it in my neck,

and she looks down at me in question. "What do you mean? I left school after my last conference and came here to wait for you. I figured you'd probably be a while since, you know, it was Tabitha."

"I went back to your room after I talked Tabitha out of going to complain to the principal and you weren't there. That fucked with my head, Hails. Don't ever do that to me again. I thought you would never speak to me again."

This isn't a conversation we should be having in the hallway for everyone to hear, so I make my way over to my door and struggle to get the keys out of my pocket with the way Hailey is clinging to me. Once I get the door open, I walk over and sit on the couch. The position is reminiscent of the first night she let me touch her in her apartment. That was after some drama too. I hope our lives aren't destined to be full of drama. I hate that shit.

Hailey picks up the conversation like it never stopped in the hall. "Mitchell." Her hands come up to cup my cheeks, forcing my eyes to stay on hers. They're soft and warm, so looking at them is *not* a hardship. "I wouldn't stop talking to you just because your ex-wife is a bitch."

"Yeah?"

She kisses me quickly. "*Yes.* Besides, we should have known better than to dry hump on my desk in the middle of an elementary school."

"I don't remember any humping. Maybe we should recreate it to be sure."

Her eyes roll and she blows out an exasperated breath. "You know what I mean."

"I love you." The words are out before I consciously know I'm going to say them and Hailey freezes above me, eyes wide and her mouth dropped open in shock. I lean forward and kiss said open mouth before dropping back so I'm almost lying on the couch. Her body follows so she's practically lying on top of me, and trust me, that's not a problem.

Her eyes are darting back and forth from one of mine to the other like she's not sure I know what I just said. I do. Believe me, I do. "You love me?" she whispers, like saying it out loud will make me take it back.

"I love you," I confirm.

Her mouth breaks into a huge smile and she laughs, kissing me at the same time.

"I love you too. So freaking much."

Now I have to laugh because she sounds like the teenager she definitely is not when she says it. I take over the kiss, wanting to lose myself in her and forget the last hour even happened. Besides, pretty soon I'll have to go get my kids from my parents and she'll have to go get Connor from daycare. Might as well take advantage of the alone time while we have it.

With that thought in mind, I throw her onto her back on the couch, covering her with my body. "Let me show you just how much I love you."

EPILOGUE

Eight months later

Mitchell

*I*t's amazing the difference only a few months makes. If someone told me a year ago that my life would change the way it has in such a short amount of time, I would've told them they were crazy.

Hailey's sitting at the breakfast bar in my apartment helping Connor finish cutting his pancakes so he can eat. We have plans this morning, plans that mean all three kids will be going to my sister's house in a few minutes. I need him to hurry up, not take a year to eat like he does sometimes.

Forty-five minutes later, all three kids are gone and Hailey and I are in my truck, headed to look at the first of three houses we found online. Yes, that's right. We're looking at houses… to purchase together. I'm tired of her sleeping on the other side of the complex some nights. I want her in bed with me every night, not just some of them.

She's picked three houses she wants to look at, but I'm pretty sure the first one is going to be the one she picks. The other two are very modern and upscale looking inside, and that's just not Hailey. It's not either of us. From the pictures online, the one has an all-white kitchen beside a mudroom, and with the amount of grease I have on my clothes and body when I get home from the garage, there's no way I'm not going to ruin the pristine counter-tops the day after we move in.

We pull up to the first house and I can already tell Hailey's in love with it. She bounces out of the car and stands at the edge of the walkway, hands clasped beneath her chin and practically emulating the heart-eyes emoji.

I walk around the car and take her hand. "Let's go look at it." She looks up at me with a huge grin on her face and nods.

"Yes, let's."

The agent is already waiting for us at the door when we reach it, and she leads us inside, waxing poetic about all the features of the house. From the front, it looked like one story, but now that we're inside I can see a staircase off to one side of the living room that leads to a second level.

Hailey wanders through the main floor, trailing her fingers along the fireplace mantle in the living room before heading into the kitchen to explore there. The room is bright and airy, with a huge fridge and a big island in the middle that houses the stove. You can see straight into the living room from the island, and Hailey tells me, "That will make cooking with Connor around a lot less dangerous."

She's already talking like it's our house. Stepping over to the large farmhouse sink, she stares out the windows at all the lush greenery. I walk up to stand behind her and look out over the big back yard. There's plenty of room out there for the kids to play, and there's a deck right outside the sliding glass doors in the dining area that I'm sure will get a lot of use.

I expect her to walk out there and look around, but she continues back through the house, visiting what looks to be the master bedroom with a bath and another bedroom. There are also two more bedrooms upstairs and surprisingly, a fifth on the lowest level. That one I'm sure Ben will claim for his own.

Finally, we make our way out onto the deck and the view is the best thing I've seen aside from Hailey. She's only out there a second before she says, "This is the one, Mitchell. I want this house."

Wrapping my arms around her, I pull her into me and laugh. "I knew you would. I don't know why you wanted to go look at those other two. They aren't us."

She laughs, pushing me away before turning to look back out at the trees behind what will be our new house. This is my chance, I know it, so when she turns back to face me, her face lit up with happiness, I'm down on one knee, a pale blue box in my hand. Hailey gasps, covering her mouth with both hands.

"Hailey Nicole Lucas. You came into my life like a hurricane, shaking everything I knew upside down and changing my life for the better. I can't imagine doing this without you, and I never want to find out what that would be like. I love you more than life. Will you marry me?"

The realtor, Meghan, who knew I was going to do this, is holding my phone, videotaping what's happening so Hailey can play it for her parents and mine later, and probably Evie too. That child will be so mad she wasn't here to see this, especially since she went with me yesterday to pick it out.

Nodding and crying, Hailey finally manages to say yes, then throws herself into my arms, knocking me back on my ass. She plants kisses all over my face as she says, "Yes," over and over and over again.

Once she finally calms, I slide the ring down her finger and she holds up her hand between us so she can look at it. "It's the most beautiful ring I've ever seen."

"I'm glad you like it since you'll be wearing it forever." Yeah, I'm being cocky, but it's the truth. I won't ever do anything to make her want to take it off. We both made mistakes when we were younger, but this time we definitely got things right.

THE WITH ME IN SEATTLE UNIVERSE

To learn more about The With Me in Seattle Universe, click here:

https://www.ladybosspress.com/with-me-in-seattle

ABOUT THE AUTHOR

Stacey is the New York Times & USA Today Bestselling Author of Second Chances, Shadows of the Past (co-authored with H.M. Ward), the Nashville Secrets series, and the Nashville U series.

She's also the single mom of three amazingly crazy boys and since she's a transplanted Yankee, considers herself a big city girl living in a small town. Because she can't live in the cities she loves – Nashville, New York, Chicago – she writes about people who do instead. When she isn't writing, you can usually find her curled up with a sexy book, or more accurately, scrolling through Tumblr. She also isn't afraid to admit her favorite addictions: Tumblr GIF's, social media, Spotify, Dr. Pepper, and of course, dirty books. Hunky heroes with control issues and strong heroines who stand up to them are her weakness. She loves to talk books – not just her own – with anyone, so send her a message!

Want to know what's coming next? Sign up for her Newsletter to be the first to hear up new releases, sales and get exclusive content too!

Where you can find her:

staceylewis.com

facebook.com/AuthorStaceyLewis

twitter.com/staceylewisauth

instagram.com/authorstaceylewis

amazon.com/author/staceylewis

bookbub.com/authors/stacey-lewis

goodreads.com/staceymosteller

pinterest.com/authorstaceylewis

.

Made in the USA
Monee, IL
25 September 2020